C000118748

HUNT THE KILLER

By the same author:

Wherein Lies Justice?, Book Guild Publishing, 2013

Staying Alive, Book Guild Publishing, 2014

HUNT THE KILLER

Barry Johnson

Book Guild Publishing

Sussex, England

First published in Great Britain in 2014 by
The Book Guild Ltd
The Werks
45 Church Road
Hove, BN3 2BE

Typesetting in Baskerville by
YHT Ltd, London

Printed and bound in Great Britain by
CPI Group (UK) Ltd, Croydon, CR0 4YY

A catalogue record for this book is available from
The British Library.

ISBN 978 1 909984 19 6

'Very interesting, Celia Foley is a corporal who works with Sergeant Billinghurst and they're close friends.'

'So it could have been either of them who visited Jase but it was probably Josey because she knows him – but why hide her identity?'

'Do you have any idea why she might have visited him?'

'In the Colchester or Peasmarsh prison?'

'Either.'

'Apart from the fact that he was innocent and shouldn't have been in prison? No.'

'When was the last time you saw her?'

'Months ago. It was when she brought the reports to be signed.'

'Any contact with her?'

'Yes, I sent her a birthday card. I sent it to Bulford and I got a reply, a thank you, from Iraq.'

'When?'

'It was after the first trial and before I went to Bolivia.'

Gaygan turned to Kitty and raised his eyebrows. She nodded. Clearly she'd just agreed to something and she continued.

3

'Jake,' she paused; it was a long, long pause, a reluctance to speak, or she was sorting out what to say.

I had a sinking feeling. It was the way she said 'Jake'. Drawn out, with a quaver in it. Her expression, the way she looked down, then up into my eyes. The pain started in the pit of my stomach. The pause, the long, long pause; my head was screaming get on with it.

'Jake... do you have any idea why anybody would have her killed?'

It was like being hit with a rock. All the breath went out of my body and my head was spinning. I couldn't speak. Why the hell would anybody kill Josey?

'Clearly a shock, Jake.'

I was dizzy, my mouth was dry and I was having difficulty breathing. I'd worked closely with this woman. She was my sergeant and we'd been in some very, very sticky situations together.

Kitty waited and then said, 'Let me give you some more information. She was shot two days after you were released from Peasmarsh, this may be coincidence, and Corporal Celia Foley is missing, AWOL. She also went absent at about the time you were released from Peasmarsh.'

This made no sense to me. I tried to think clearly. Did they think I'd killed her? No. I'd tried to see Jase and I couldn't get a visitor's pass, but Josey did or now it seemed it really was Celia Foley. Jase and Josey then get killed. I get released from prison – and Celia Foley disappears. This whole thing was daft. What was so important that there were a plague of murders? Was Celia Foley also a target?

Kitty went to speak. I cut her off. The conclusion, I assumed, was that Josey passed information to Jase or he passed information to her. How was Celia involved? But why wait until they'd met? If it was suspected they had some information, kill them. Perhaps the meeting and the killings were not connected. No, that's about as likely as a virgin birth. I'd no idea what was going on. I tried to clear my head.

'I think you've established that I know nothing about whatever theory you have. How about telling me what you do have.'

Kitty went to speak. I cut her off again. I needed to open this up.

'Has anybody else been killed who may be connected?'

Kitty nodded. 'Do you know of a woman named Mary Telford?'

'No.'

'She was a do-gooder, supplying food and blankets to the displaced in Iraq in one of the camps. She went out with Phillips. The American MPs interviewed Mary Telford when an Iraqi woman she worked with was murdered. It seems she suggested the killer was a certain major in the British Army. She came home and was killed just before you were released. Same MO as Sergeant Billinghurst, same lack of evidence.'

'Did Jase know her?'

'Yes, we believe so.'

'So, Jase passed information to Mary Telford or she passed information to him.'

'Seems a sound theory.' Kitty paused, 'Okay, you knew Sergeant Billinghurst was working with the Americans on the murder of two Iraqi women. One of them worked with

Mary Telford. The investigation was apparently going nowhere but that's no surprise given they were in what amounted to a war zone.'

'Can I just ask a question here? The murdered Iraqi women; were they killed in the same way as Mary Telford.'

'No. Mary Telford was shot. The Iraqi women were raped and strangled.'

'So definitely different killers?'

'We think so. Different method, different country.'

'Okay.' I waited for Kitty to continue.

'You were in hospital waiting to be flown home and your Sergeant Billinghurst visited a certain Sergeant Phillips who was in custody.'

'This was in Iraq?'

'Yes, in Iraq. We don't know what triggered that meeting or why she went. What we do know was when she got back with the Americans she suggested that perhaps the murderer was a serial killer and perhaps there were similar killings in the UK and US.'

'Wooh! You're suggesting that Jase gave her a lead or at least an idea that there were other killings.'

'We thought that may be the case so we asked the Americans for the investigation notes. That was a no-no, but they did talk to us. The investigating team thought it was the case because they didn't bugger about. The Americans instituted a search of cases in the States and the British did the same in the UK. Four cases came up in the UK.'

'Let me just get this right. Two Iraqi women from the US sector were murdered in the UK sector. One of them worked with a Mary Telford. Jase kills Major Carmichael. I get injured and end up in hospital. Josey gets loaned to the American military police. She has a meeting with Jase. Either Josey or Mary Telford suggest that there may be more killings in the US or UK. Four are identified in the UK. Do we have a timeline on those?'

'Well no, it wasn't our case.'

'So we have to get that.'

'Why?'

'Well, if we know when the Iraqis were killed in Iraq and we know when women were killed in the UK we will know who is the likely killer. What about the Yanks?'

'They stopped their enquiry.'

Kitty turned to Gaygan. 'I'm on my way,' he said. 'You want the dates of the killings and what military personnel and those connected to the military were both in the UK and in Iraq when the killings occurred.' She smiled. Gaygan was definitely switched on.

'Oh and give DCI Rod Wilkes a ring, find out why the Americans called off their search.'

'How are you going to get that information, Gaygan?' I asked.

'I don't know yet.'

'You get the dates and then I will make a call to the MOD and that should give us the names.' Gaygan nodded and left.

'Where did we get to?' I asked.

'You summarising the killings,' said Kitty.

'Right, Mary Telford is killed, Jase is stabbed, Josey is shot and RMP Corporal Celia Foley goes AWOL.'

'This is a dog's breakfast, Jake.'

'Let me get a different perspective. I'll get a conversation with Mabry.'

'The Home Secretary? Why? Can you...'

'He helped get me into Peasmarsh Prison to try and sort out the Jason Phillips killing. Remember Jase killed Carmichael so Mabry might know something.'

'Thank you, Jake.' Kitty stood. 'I'll think about what we have discussed and come and see you tomorrow. I must be going.' She kissed me on the cheek and hurried out.

13

4

I phoned Barrow and told Pauline, his secretary, that I would like to talk to Mabry. Twenty minutes later, whilst spread-eagled on the settee, thinking about the day, Purdy sitting on my chest, the phone went. It was just out of reach so I rolled to get it and Purdy jumped off me, tail erect and fluffed up, she stalked across the room to an armchair and pointedly ignored me as she athletically bounced onto the seat and curled up. It was Pauline with a message from Mabry. It had come via Charles, Mabry's personal assistant. How extraordinary, perhaps it's telepathy. I laughed at myself. Mabry, it seemed, wanted feedback on what had happened in prison and had arranged dinner in a restaurant in London. This was odd as all our meetings before had been at the Home Office or Portcullis House. It also seemed strange that Charles phoned the message to Barrow's offices, Mabry always contacted me direct; he never let his left hand know what his right hand was doing, and we didn't have an eating together relationship.

Because of the pattern change I had Pauline transfer me to Barrow. He was cautious.

'Okay, Jake.' He paused. 'You will go this evening unarmed. Nikki will be with you as your bodyguard.'

Seemed good to me. If you need protection it's best to take the best hitman in the UK, even if Nikki was a woman and a very attractive woman at that.

Sam came in from work and fussed. She was, as you might

14

'Okay, got it.'

'In reality, she went to the restaurant and other guests were there but not Mabry. She didn't go in but has the names. I think you should stay away from her.'

'Why?'

'She's a bad influence.' And with that she reached across the covers and squeezed, accurately and painfully.

'Yes my lovely.' She released. 'Are you okay?' I swallowed. She smiled.

'Apart from being here for hours worried about you and waiting while they dug a bullet out of you and watching them pump gallons of blood into you and generally wondering what most of the staff do here apart from wandering about chatting about holidays, supper tonight and moaning about the management, I'm fine.' She paused. I knew it was coming. She does that: says something, pauses and then has a little dig. 'Do you know that about eighty per cent of the time we've been together you've been in prison in America or in prison here or in hospital?'

'I'm sorry, it's just the way things turned out.'

'I know, but when I get you home you're going to stay there for a while.'

'Okay, my lovely. You've a deal. Could you get the medics and the coppers? I have to get out of here.'

'No, you bloody stay there.' She smiled. 'I'll leave you to their tender mercies. Then I'll come and beat you up myself.'

Sam left and she was gone for a while. I just lay there; my life had changed dramatically, not least in having Sam living with me. I'd joined the MI5 Special Unit as an investigator and I knew two others were assassins, my boss Frances, who had been killed by the Mafia, and Nikki, but it was a while before I recognised that. I also knew they were all investigators apart from Howard, who had been recruited as a planner and still was a planner, the best one I'd ever come

19

across. Now I was clear; I was also a killer. It didn't worry me. I suppose Barrow had recognised that when he recruited me; and me being a military police captain and recognising the need in the hot situation of war does give you a certain orientation. The Bolivian experience, when it was only a question of just trying to stay alive and killing out of sheer necessity, confirmed that I had what it took to kill without losing sleep over it. Killing Ratty in prison had been different, though. He'd killed Jase, and Barrow had intimated it was okay for me to kill Jase's killer, but he'd never ordered me to do that. My kills were mounting up. The questions by Frances at my acceptance interview did indicate the route my special unit career was likely to take, but I never thought I'd be able to accept killing a real, live, breathing human being so readily. I suppose the James Bond books and the licence to kill thing had amused me. I now knew that there was a similar unit hidden away under the cover of MI6 and they operated very differently from us. They were individuals and we operated as a team. The nagging question was, was I sane? I wondered why the special unit boss, Barrow, was a psychiatrist, though he was more of a psychotherapist than a medic. He was a great leader but did he have that specialist knowledge and understanding to see if we were tipping over the edge or was the idea that killing is not unnatural but just a social norm to enable civilisation? Well, I felt sane so that must have been good enough or perhaps if you feel sane, you're not. I heard movement in the corridor. Perhaps reality is about to strike.

I must admit to being surprised when in walked Detective Chief Inspector Wilkes, who was in the Serious and Organised Crime Directorate. He'd been the man that warned me that Jase Phillips and Mike Munro were about to be stitched up at their court martial. With him was Kitty Halloway.

'My word, not the local friendly Bobbies but you two, and

'Why did they pull out?'

'They said it was a British problem.' She was frowning.

'But they must know that just one case in the States would identify the culprit.'

'You're right, Jake, and we believe we know who it is but we need the last piece of the jigsaw that eliminates six hundred and one people.'

There was a silence in the room. I looked at the faces. Kitty was looking at the ceiling, her bottom lip was pushing up over her top lip and Rod had his hands clasped and was looking down at them. I smiled. We were all thinking the same thing. I couldn't resist it; I had to ask.

'I wonder why the Americans pulled out.'

Rod gave a little cough.

'Well, what is it?'

'It could be a high-level blocking run.'

'Could it, Rob? The Family?'

He fidgeted in his seat. Kitty looked at him and shook her head.

'Or it could be their military. Barrow wants you to go and talk to the FBI,' Kitty said to me.

'That might slow things down, but I won't be out of here for a couple of days and then I'll need to get well enough to travel to the States. Can I just recap? What exactly are you investigating now, the killing of Josey and the attack on me or some suspected serial killings?'

'Well, we were called in on the Josey case because the locals in Salisbury recognised this had a mix of things, military killing on their patch. Then we get this whole plot of connections to Iraq, perhaps serial killing, and my boss got bounced and provided us to do that as well requested MI5 help and as you knew Sergeant Billinghurst and you were in the RMP ... it just happened.'

'It just happened that you knew me?'

'Yes, well, you got away with it last time, this time I can watch you if you decide to bump someone off.'

'Look we have two cases here with perhaps some links but they are separate. You have the killings of Josey and Mary Telford, the shooting of me and an AWOL that may be connected and you have suggested serial killings that are perhaps separate. Let's nail down one and then have a crack at the other.'

'Okay.'

'When was Josey killed?'

'Last week, Tuesday.'

'When were the serial killings?'

'Oh, when you were in Iraq.'

'That was months ago. Okay, let's tackle the Josey case and see where that takes us.'

Rod said, 'Can I leave you two to go over the murder of Sergeant Billinghurst and what we've deduced so far? I need to be away.' With that, Chief Inspector Rod Wilkes left. Kitty looked at me, her expression was one of understanding. I nodded. Rod wanted to be strictly below the parapet when it came to Family matters.

'Now we can really talk, Jake.'

'Problem?' I asked.

'Not really. Rod's a nice guy but he has no real criminal investigation experience. He does have loads of political and media contacts, though. Not that we need that right now. He'll probably be useful when we have to negotiate our way through the political minefield.'

'Only if he stops hiding. Okay, what have you got?'

'Hiding?'

'You saw it.'

'He has a fear of The Family?'

'Right; if there's any hint they might be involved he disappears.'

'He couldn't be a member?'

'No. West is their man but I'm sure there are others.'

'He's a superintendent?'

'Right, Home Office liaison.'

'Okay, Jake, let's start at what I think was the beginning. Josey Billinghurst was working with the Americans on the murder of two Iraqi women. She visits Jason Phillips and, whoops, the question comes up that perhaps this is a serial killer they're looking for. The idea also seemed to be that it's a soldier, and a British soldier at that.'

'British soldier? This is speculation, Kitty. You've no evidence.'

'True. Both the Americans and us do a search. In the UK four similar deaths come up complete with dates and places. All prior to the Iraqi killings.'

'You going to tell me why you think it's a Brit?'

'Only because of the Mary Telford suggestion and because Jason Phillips is involved and he's in the British Army, he's talked to Sergeant Billinghurst and he knows about the British killings. Your Sergeant Billinghurst has stayed with the case and didn't push it back at the Americans and she is the one who's been killed.'

'How would Jase know about the British killings?'

We both said together, 'Sergeant Billinghurst,' and we laughed.

'All we need now is some solid evidence about any of this,' I said. 'As a tentative first step the motivation could be a knowledge of the Iraqi murders and a certain major being suggested as the killer. I think that's related to Josey's and Mary's killing, and my shooting.'

'What we really need,' she paused, nodding as she beat the fingers of her right hand on to the palm of her left hand, 'is to find out who hired the hitman who killed Josey Billinghurst, Mary Telford and nearly got you – assuming it was in fact the same person.' She gave an emphatic nod. She was clear where we had to go.

27

It seemed to me we'd lots of confusing or confused information, but Occam's Razor, the idea that when you've more than one theory the simplest one is probably correct, suggested to me that Carmichael was the killer and Jase believed that, and because he believed that he shared it with Josey and Mary Telford and all three were killed, and as I'd been working with Josey an attempt was made on my life and as Celia Foley was a friend of Josey she was AWOL. So is she alive? I had a little warning buzzing in my brain. This fits together neatly but that doesn't make it right. What we needed now was some evidence.

'Okay, let's follow the Josey killing.' At least now we had some boundaries on where we were going.

7

The nurse came back in.

'Excuse me, madam, I'm afraid you will have to leave.'

'Oh, why?'

'This patient is to be moved to another hospital.'

'Where?'

'I don't know, madam, but we need to prepare him to be moved.'

A man who said he was Doctor Street came in, complete with a team of two. With the nurse they uncoupled me from the medical equipment and reconnected me to the equipment on a trolley. They were slick, efficient and silent. The efficiency just blew me away. I asked Doctor Street where I was going. He smiled.

'Lancaster Nightingale. It is a private hospital and Barrow, I think he is your boss, said he will see you there tomorrow.' I'd never heard of this hospital but that was no surprise; I can't say that I am particularly interested in hospitals. I should have realised there was a problem as in that situation, a doctor wouldn't have said Barrow, but would have said Sir Barrow Jones. I was just not switched on.

'Why the move?'

'He said it was for security.'

I watched Kitty speak to the doctor and she made a note in her notebook.

'Bye then, Jake. I'll catch up with you in your new abode.'

Did I detect something in her voice? Perhaps she was worried about me.

In less than fifteen minutes we were on our way. The efficiency was incredible, hardly NHS, as was the silence of the staff moving me. No chatter, just effective efficiency. Soon I knew we were on the motorway. It was the regular thump of the road as we crossed the tarred joints in the concrete and the steady engine noise of cars passing us on the right and us passing cars and lorries on the left. The two medics were with me in the back. We were bombing along.

I dozed, there's not much to do lying in an ambulance, strapped in, hooked up to a drip and my vital signs being monitored, although I thought this was excessive. Blues and twos woke me. I thought it was the ambulance and then realised it was coming from behind us and I could see the blues flashing in the windows. I realised the ambulance had speeded up and was rocking and its blues and twos were now flashing and sounding.

One of the men drew a gun and the other shouted at him to put it away.

'He can recognise us.'

'Tom, put it away, she wants him alive.' Tom reluctantly holstered his weapon. So a woman ordered this. I wondered who.

We veered to the left and I rocked against the straps holding me and the two medics were hanging on. We were going up a steep incline, I thought it must be an intersection, and then we were weaving and did what seemed to be an emergency stop as I violently jerked forwards on the stretcher. The medics jumped out. I had the impression we were in a car park. I realised it must be a motorway service station.

I heard shouts and a uniformed police officer came through the open ambulance door.

'Mr Robinson?' he said. I agreed. He smiled. 'I've never

chased an ambulance before and he could certainly drive.' I really couldn't think of anything to say. It had been like riding on a fairground rollercoaster as a kid, sort of exciting and concerning at not being in control. 'We'll get you back to hospital. The engine is still running so they must have left the keys.' Kitty appeared.

'Oh, good afternoon Detective Inspector, fancy you letting me be kidnapped.'

'Silence, Jake Robinson, or I will arrest you for absconding from hospital and stealing a ride in an ambulance.' The uniformed police officer just grinned.

Half an hour later we were heading back down the motorway, having been checked out by a local doctor. This time two real medics were with me and I was disconnected from the equipment as it was deemed unnecessary by the doctor. In fact he said I could sit up.

I wasn't sure what it had all been about but Kitty had smelt a rat and thrown up some alert and spoken to Barrow's secretary.

Safely reinstalled in the hospital, without connection to the medical paraphernalia, and guarded by police officers, Kitty came to visit me.

'What was that all about then, Kitty?'

'The local police are dealing with it and will give me a full briefing. They have two of the four men but they are not talking, have no criminal records and said they were just hired for the job and thought it was kosher but they are ex-Royal Army Medical Corps.'

'They were armed?'

'Not when the locals caught up with them. If I get anything I will tell you. I won't come in tomorrow, I have some chasing to do, but Thursday we will pick up where we left off.'

'Let's see if we can get some tea. Is Sam here?'

'Christ, I'm sorry, Jake.'

31

Kitty set off and came back with Sam, who had a tray of tea and buns. A nurse then came in and gave me a hard time about getting crumbs in the bed before I had a chance to get any crumbs in the bed, stuck a thermometer in my ear, made me take some pills and then disappeared. My mum used to stick a thermometer under my tongue and tell me not to bite it and she used to stick it up my young brother's bum, but sticking it in my ear just didn't seem right. Kitty made an excuse and disappeared. Perhaps a thermometer in my ear embarrassed her.

'Where have you been?'

'Didn't anybody tell you?'

'Well, they said you were going to another hospital and then they said you had been abducted. Then you arrive back here and I haven't even been home.'

'Still, we are both here now.' She knew I was playing it all down, but there was no reason not to.

'You two seem to be getting on very well,' Sam said.

'I'm sorry, my lovely, but a police officer I worked with in Iraq has been murdered and it turns out she was investigating a string of killings.'

'Was your shooting related?' I could hear that she wanted me to say no, and she was very still and stiff.

'It may have been.'

'And this abduction?'

'It may have been.'

I had this uneasy concern. Sam sat quietly looking at me. Her face was expressionless. She was thinking and I had no idea what was going through her head.

'You're worried about me, aren't you?' She had read my concern.

'Sam, we don't know what we're dealing with here but I think I need you protected, just in case.'

'Just in case of what?'

32

'Just in case whoever this is tries to get at me through you.'

'You mean kill me?' She was about to laugh, and didn't. 'Don't be daft...' Her voice petered out. 'You mean it, don't you?' There was still a lack of belief. I suppose people who live in a normal world think that the sort of person I am could only be a character on TV.

'I'm going to make a phone call and have Barrow get someone to look after you.'

'Not your girlfriend, Nikki.'

'No, she might be too expensive.' I laughed.

'Well, she's downstairs now. Barrow sent her to guard you. All the men in this place are finding excuses to walk past where she's sitting.'

'Have you been sitting with her?'

'Well, yes.'

'I see! When you go just send her up to hold my hand, or um-'

'You bastard.' She hit me with a series of pretend slaps just as Kitty came back in the room.

''Allo, 'allo, 'allo, do I observe violence towards one of the patients of this 'ere 'ospital?'

'Kitty, please ring Barrow and get your sergeant to take Sam to wherever he says she should be taken. Protective custody at Holloway might be good. You could arrest her and have her imprisoned properly.' I was holding Sam.

'I'm not surprised some nice person tried to kill you,' said Sam, but then she kissed me.

'Sam...'

'Oh Jake, stop pissing about.' She was looking at me uncertainly. She really wanted me to have been kidding but was uncertain and now reality was seeping into her thoughts. She pulled her head back and was staring at me.

'Sam, let Barrow assess the risk and take the appropriate actions.'

As we were talking Kitty had taken out her phone. 'Yes, Barrow, my sergeant will stay with her until she arrives and Nikki can shove off as she's affecting the blood pressure of the male staff here,' she was saying. 'Okay, Barrow.'

'Until who arrives?' asked Sam.

'A lady named Ethel.'

'Ethel?' Sam's disbelief returned and she laughed.

Sam and I looked at Kitty. 'Yes, she's a specialist protection officer, covert security, MI5. She'll be staying with you for a few days.'

Sam looked at me and shook her head. 'I've only been with you a few months and now my life's in danger so I have to have a bodyguard and her name's Ethel and don't you dare say sorry.' There was a touch of anger in her voice but also understanding and amusement.

I started to laugh and she came over, kissed me on the lips, turned to Kitty and said, 'Well! Where's this sergeant then? I hope he's better looking than this.' She pointed at me and the two women left. About twenty minutes later, Kitty came back with more tea and this time biscuits.

'Jake Robinson, you're the luckiest bastard in the world.' I wondered what she was talking about. She must have seen the expression on my face. 'Most men would give their left testicle for a woman like that.'

'Um, I'm not sure they'd go that far.'

'Well I am. When I introduced her to Gaygan he thought he'd died and gone to heaven or whatever the Hindu equivalent is.'

'Thank you, Kitty, for your insights into the needs and lusts of the male of the species. Now, let's deal with Josey's murder. Tell me the where, when, how and all that stuff.'

'I think we'd best go there.'

'Get me released from this place.'

Kitty disappeared and came back with a grin like the Cheshire cat. 'Tomorrow morning. They will bandage you

where this Muna is and she seems to think Muna's with Malc. I assume that's Wright.'

'Why did he send it to Celia?'

'This is from before Jase was sentenced and he's asking Celia what she can find out.'

'And has she found anything?'

'No, I don't think so. There's no record of a reply but she might have just told him if she found anything.'

'It might be worth following up.' Celia was still AWOL so we couldn't follow up with her, we would have to sit on it until we found her.

9

As things turned out, I didn't go to the States. I went to the MOD in London and met up with Lieutenant Colonel Willaby-Alexander.

'So, Captain, according to Sir Barrow you're back chasing military killers and want the locations of some soldiers tracked. Who was murdered this time?'

'Sergeant Josephine Billinghurst, sir, but I'm more interested in a soldier who has killed a number of people.'

'I know that name. Yes.' The colonel seemed to be off beam, almost as if he didn't hear my last sentence. He was looking up with a faraway expression on his face. He looked at me and it seemed the memory came. 'She was military police, wasn't she?' He nodded. The conversation was all questions with the colonel. Luckily, most of them were rhetorical. 'Yes, I remember, worked with you on the Carmichael case, didn't she? Must be difficult when it's one of your own killed, eh?'

No, he hadn't registered what I was really looking for. How odd. No, not odd really, my grandmother was like that. She would get stuck with one idea at a time but the colonel's too young to have Alzheimer's.

'Yes, sir.'

'So what do you want?' The question was asked as if he had no idea why I was there.

'We believe that, of a list of names that we have, some may have been in the United States in the past couple of years. If

42

any were there then we could give the dates to the FBI and they can do a survey of murders and if they find one that matches the profile that may tell us the killer. That in turn would narrow down our search for suspects not only to the original murders but it may lead us to who killed Sergeant Billinghurst. This is highly confidential, sir. I'm fishing at the moment.'

'Understood, Captain. Means the searchers mustn't know what you're really looking for, yes?'

'Yes, sir.'

'Can I introduce you to somebody who can help?'

He was back to his normal self. We went through a myriad of corridors with glossy floors that smelled of institutional polish. I could imagine the manufacturers had people working on getting the smell just right for a particular establishment, so the MOD would smell different from the House of Lords. Eventually, we arrived at a huge room full of people at computers. It was quiet. Some were using tele-phones but had headsets on, so I suppose the ringtone was in the headset. Around the desks or groups of desks were sound-absorbent barriers. The floor was carpeted and the ceiling had acoustic tiles. A few people were talking but quietly. It was a soulless place with all the trappings of being environmentally designed: a modern hell. I had the feeling you could die of loneliness in here and no one would know. Modern slavery takes a different form from ancient slavery. Perhaps it's my level of freedom that causes me to think this way.

The colonel wove his way through the stations of people, focussing on an immediate task, until he came to one occupied by a slim, dark-haired woman who was slightly separated from the rest. She had two visitors' chairs within her enclosure.

'Lucy, this is, is…' He paused, looked at me and recog-nition came into his eyes. 'Captain Robinson. I think you

43

may be able to help him. He has a long list of names and wants to know if any of them has visited the USA recently. I can't tell you why he wants to know but it's pretty important.'

'Yes, Colonel.' She turned her dark, curious eyes on me. 'How do you do, Captain.' She smiled, an attractive, come-hither smile.

'I'll leave you two with it, shall I? Goodbye, Captain. You'll let me know how you get on with Lucy, won't you?' He smiled and nodded. The question hung in the air.

'Yes, sir.'

The colonel turned and weaved his way through the islands of slaves.

'So, about this list, Captain.'

'Is the colonel okay?' I asked.

'He's going to retire soon, sometimes forgets things. I like him. He used to be fun but he worries now. He's unsure, where he used to be so positive.' She paused then became business-like and said. 'Now, Captain, what is it you want?'

'I've a list of six hundred and two names. A lot of them are civilians and many are American service personnel, so you probably can't help me with those. I want to know if any of them were in the USA in the period six months ago to two years six months ago. For the military personnel, I've the names, ranks and numbers on a disc.'

'Thank goodness for that.' I could hear the relief in her voice. 'Let me set up a search program. I can only tell you if they were in the USA officially. We wouldn't know if they travelled to the USA privately. Are you interested in whether they went to any other countries?'

'We know they were all in Iraq during that period.'

'If they were military contractors, Jane may be able to help you, but I'll have to get back to you on that and we may have a few Americans. Let me show you where all the military ones were by country.'

44

mischievous way. 'I won't let Sam know but it might cost you.'

What had I done to deserve this hassle?

'We'll be round within the hour,' I told Lucy and rang off.

'We?' said Kitty knowingly.

'Yes, bloody we.'

'Okay, okay! No need to get niggy.' She smiled. 'I really do understand that you need protection. After all, you being a heroic soldier and all and she's going to have *everything* ready.' I decided to ignore her game.

It took about twenty minutes to get to the MOD and then another half hour to gain entry. It was no problem for me – my MI5 credentials were sufficient and anyway, I was on their security computer – but Kitty's warrant card cut no ice and we had to see a man who had to check with another man and eventually we were in and up to see Lucy.

'Hi, Lucy.'

She spun round in her chair with a big smile when she heard my voice, which died as she saw Kitty. 'And you are?' It wasn't exactly an unfriendly question as unexpected.

'Detective Inspector Halloway, Murder Squad, Metropolitan Police.'

'Oh my. I didn't know this was about murder.'

'Oh yes, it's about murder and more than that. I've a role in protecting Jake.'

Lucy laughed. Her bubbly good humour had returned. 'I didn't intend to kill him, well not unless he has a dicky ticker. Still, one never knows, does one?'

Both women laughed. Clearly they'd reached an understanding that was beyond the grasp of any normal man.

'Would you excuse me for a moment?' she then asked. 'I just need to check something.' She left and we waited about ten minutes before she returned. 'Good, I can now give you the information. Would you like to inspect the findings, Captain? Inspector?'

I had a feeling that she'd gone to check on Kitty. She then swung the screen on the swivel mounting and pointed to two chairs all at the same time. We sat.

'I'll work through each of your – I'm not sure if they're suspects – the names that you've given me. Let's start at the top, with Major Carmichael, now deceased.'

The screen filled with information. This was filtered down until only about ten lines were on the screen.

'As you can see he was in Washington in the April before he went back to Iraq. He actually went to the Pentagon. The reason for his visit seems to have been his acceptance of a role there as a lieutenant colonel on the staff of an American General with some form of strategic role. The exact nature of the department is classified but what I can say is that the officer he was replacing was a full colonel who had been promoted to general, so your major was on a very fast track. Off the record, and I didn't say this, but the only other two people I've seen with the career pattern of Major Carmichael had high level, shall we call it, "clout" backing them. Clearly he'd been selected for big things. I had a word with your friend Colonel Willaby-Alexander because there were some minor anomalies and he agreed with me.'

'About what?'

'Well, your Major Carmichael had a fantastic action record. He dived in where normal heroes feared to tread. He was one very brave and very lucky man. The reports indicate that he'd take enormous risks and had the luck of the devil in pulling them off.'

'It could be that he was a bloody good soldier.'

'It could, but reading between the lines his commanders didn't think so. Looking at the paperwork, he should have had a chest full of gallantry medals but he only had one, a DSC, and the Navy gave him that one.'

Kitty asked, 'Should you be telling us this?'

'Good question! I've just cleared this stuff upstairs to

make sure you were kosher. Commander Philpot vouched for the captain and said I should be open with him. You seem to have some extraordinary contacts, Captain.'

Kitty looked at me. There was a question hovering. She turned to Lucy. 'What do you mean by that?'

'Well, Commander Philpot is a high flier in the Navy security area and he said the captain is okay but made a call and checked you out with TNT, Inspector.'

'TNT?'

Lucy laughed. 'Sir Antony Newham-Taylor, head of MI5.'

Kitty looked bemused.

'Come on, Detective, Tony Newham-Taylor.'

Kitty fell in and laughed.

'Apparently when Commander Philpot said you were with Jake here TNT said it would be all right.'

Kitty turned to me. 'Do you really know all these people?'

I shrugged. 'Perhaps we should press on.'

'I was given security clearance just because I was with you, Jake?'

'That's exactly the point,' said Lucy.

'Christ, why the hell were you only a captain?' said Kitty. Both Kitty and Lucy were looking at me.

'Why does the sun rise in the east? Perhaps that's just the way of things.'

'Anyway,' said Lucy. 'Your man was in Washington legitimately and the two soldiers Holt and Wright were listed as staff.'

'Is that usual?' I asked.

'Not really; it's not unusual but not normal.'

Such are the mysteries of the English language that I just accepted what Lucy said. 'So, all three were there officially?'

'I suppose so.'

I assumed that was the 'not unusual but not normal' bit.

'The army paid the expenses or rather the Pentagon did,' said Lucy.

'What about the other people?'

'So we've cleared three. The others were Corporal Gil Hibberd, Sergeant Josephine Billinghurst, Sergeant Jason Phillips and Flt Lt Susan Thomas. Flt Lt Susan Thomas was easy to clear. At that time she was on the staff of an American Lieutenant General who was controlling the air logistics. This was a regular trip that just happened to occur at that time.'

'So the three oddities were Sergeant Josephine Billinghurst, Sergeant Jason Phillips and Corporal Gil Hibberd.'

'Right. Sergeant Billinghurst was there on a case. I've no information on the case and the RMP won't give me anything. All her files are closed because she's been murdered.'

'That's crazy,' said Kitty. 'It's my case.'

'I didn't know that, Inspector, but you can get the information direct.'

'That leaves Jase,' I said.

'And Corporal Gil Hibberd,' said Kitty.

'Yes, it might be worth having a chat with him.'

'Not a problem,' said Lucy. 'He's on a course in Hereford. Here's the number and there's the name of the man you'll need to contact to interview him.'

'Should you tell me this?'

'I won't tell if you don't tell,' she said with a voice full of innuendo.

Kitty cut in brusquely. 'What about Jason Phillips?'

'He requested permission to go to the States. Apparently, his wife had taken his children there and he was due to go back to Iraq. He had some leave and just got clearance to go to the States. If he'd just gone, we wouldn't have known. He just stuck to the rules.'

'Did Gil Hibberd stick to the rules?'

'Oh, yes. He was on leave and requested to visit his sister

on compassionate grounds, family business, but those grounds aren't listed.'

Well, that was that then. All were there but some follow-up was indicated. Why was Josey really in Washington? Not that she would be the killer, but there may be a link. Was Jase there to see his kids? Why would he stick to the rules? Nobody sticks to these bureaucratic rules. And Gil Hibberd just said family business. That could be meaningful. The Family? Or just family? And there were some questions to ask about Holt and Wright.

'What about Otis Brockett and Hashi Syedain?' I asked.

'They're civilians. Information is a bit vague. All it says is a business visit on behalf of Macintyre Industries.'

Kitty looked at me but it meant nothing to me.

'Let's see,' said Lucy. She then went online and looked up Macintyre Industries. It was no help at all. It was some sort of banking or finance business with the Iraqi government but what sort of banking or finance business was unclear. It seemed, reading between the lines, that they invested in the UK for clients in Iraq. I was uncomfortable as there was a reference to Charnforth Wealth Management and I knew that was a subsidiary of Whitehaven Investments, an American company with links to The Family.

'Okay, Kitty, they're Family.'

'You mean...?'

'Yes, but they won't be our targets for this crime unless lots of money is involved. They could be tied into other crime, though.'

'Such as drugs?' said Kitty.

'We'll just mark that as interesting and may be related.'

11

In the meantime, we decided to check out Gil Hibberd, so I made the call to Hereford. The major I got through to was less than happy, but after I explained he said he would ring back. This he did in less than half an hour.

'I've checked you out, Captain, and it seems you're who you say you are and security cleared. If you can get down here you can interview Corporal Hibberd at 0600 tomorrow.' It seemed to me that once again the army was reluctant to cooperate with the police. Meeting at 0600, and we have to drive across from London. He then gave me the location, which was a hotel. He also said he would be present. I was going to ask if he was security cleared but decided against.

My head was buzzing with information and when that happens there can be no solutions. Step back, Jake. Forget all about it and start again tomorrow. My thoughts told me there was a beautiful, beautiful woman waiting for me to take her out for the evening; tomorrow is another day, so I phoned the R.S. *Hispaniola* and booked a table for two. I must admit I didn't expect to get one but it was just one of those mysteries, a cancellation and we were in.

When I got home Sam thought this was a great idea so we dressed. Sam just looked stunning. Well, she always looked stunning, but for tonight she really turned it on. She was wearing a white strapless dress that hugged her curves perfectly, and went down to the bottom of her knees. The material was fabulously lightweight, that you thought you could see through, with pleated detail at the back of the bodice and back of the skirt and a broad pleated dark blue satin waistband. She wore a fine gold chain necklace with a slightly heavier similar chain on her right, a Rado watch on her left wrist and fine gold earrings. I just knew that whatever I wore I would be a scruff in comparison.

We went early on the tube to Westminster and wandered along the Victoria Embankment, past the Battle of Britain Monument and the embankment gardens. There were a few other strollers, but I had a feeling we were being tracked. Whoever it was, was good. Then I knew we were being followed and it was a relay. On the tube it had been a woman. Now it was a man, middle-aged. I said nothing to Sam. Perhaps I'm paranoid. We walked as far as Cleopatra's Needle and then wandered back, passing the Jubilee Bridge, to the Hispaniola, which is permanently moored alongside the Victoria Embankment. We arrived on board at 7.30 p.m. and so sat on the sun deck having a drink and browsing the menu. We relaxed, enjoying the fabulous view of the river, the London Eye and the Houses of Parliament. We spent some time deciding whether we would have the same thing or each have something different, and then we had to decide whether we would decide for ourselves or for each other. We rose to the challenge and decided to order for each other.

The wine waiter brought a bottle of prosecco to lubricate our decisions. I read the blurb on the label with unnecessary emphasis so we were both laughing like a pair of teenagers.

'Shall I start then, Sam?' I thought that would give her a chance to get her own back if I gave her something she didn't like. 'How about English beetroot carpaccio, goats' cheese panna cotta with dill dressing.'

'What is carpaccio?' Sam asked sipping her wine.

'Um, well, I thought it was raw meat of some description but I was intrigued by it being beetroot.'

'I see, sneaky. So you will have to have the black pudding, poached hen's egg and a Granny Smith apple.' I wasn't sure about the apple but the waiter, who was enjoying this game, thought the apple was the highlight of the starter.

Sam liked fish so I ordered for her pan-fried sea bass, red pepper piperade, sherry dressing, new potatoes and green beans and I ended up with char-grilled Orkney gold rib-eye steak, field mushroom, and plum tomato with hollandaise sauce, fries and buttered spinach. For sweet we both had praline crème brûlée. One bottle finished during the ordering, we ordered another and just enjoyed laughing at what we could see around us. The couple that really didn't want to come out to dinner and were not talking, and the young couple on what seemed like a first date, the young man clearly worried. Perhaps it was the prices or just not understanding what they had ordered. He will learn. Most of us don't understand the menu in expensive restaurants, we just treat it with a sense of adventure or ask. Sam of course was Sam, and we had more attention from more waiters than any other diners there. What I love about her is that she just doesn't notice that she acts as a human magnet drawing in the males.

We left the *Hispaniola* having had too much to drink and I was enjoying the evening; just looking at Sam I could see she was enjoying it as well. The scene was beautiful and I felt a buzz of excitement. I'm not sure what I was excited about; it was just the ambience of that evening with a new moon hanging in the clear sky, the music and above all, Sam, in her white, off-the-shoulder dress, her fair hair tumbling down and the covert glances from the other people who could see how in love we were. A tabby cat wandered with a stately stroll across a small lawn ignoring the people. He was long and slim; I just assumed the cat was a he. He glanced at me, showing his white muzzle and turned again to resume his saunter in his territory. He jumped up on a bench with ease and grace, looked at me with an arrogant stare and began to clean himself. He then stopped and again looked at me with those challenging green eyes and yawned as if to say, 'You've only got her, and she's beautiful, but I've all the she-cats in this area.' Oh, he was an egotistical bugger and because I had Sam I was as well. But all the time this romantic scene was playing out I was still aware of the tails that we couldn't shake. A woman was sitting on the wall. She'd been by the Hispaniola when we were on the deck and I wondered why we were being tracked and by whom.

12

Kitty and I set off before the sun had even decided it was near morning. I was pleased that she was driving as I was in no condition to do so and we arrived at 5.30 a.m.

As we walked in, the woman at reception asked if I was Captain Robinson. She looked at Kitty and Kitty showed her warrant card. The woman made a call and asked us to wait in the lounge where we were served coffee. There was another woman in the lounge, sitting by the window, positioned in such a way that she could see both the car park and the reception desk. I was definitely feeling paranoid; they – the ubiquitous 'they' – were watching me. No, it must have been a coincidence. How would anybody know we were coming to this hotel? A couple of minutes later, a tall, rangy, craggy-faced man in a green Harris Tweed jacket, brown corduroy trousers and heavy brogue shoes came into the reception. It was the 'I'm not really a soldier', mufti uniform again.

'Captain Robinson?'

I handed him my identification.

'No wonder you were security cleared. And you, madam?'

'Detective Inspector Halloway, Murder Squad,' she said.

'I see.' He raised his eyebrows. 'I suppose you'd better come with me then.'

We were led to a private room where Corporal Hibberd was waiting for us. I suppose it was a function room for courses run in the hotel. Corporal Hibberd was a tough-

looking, dark-skinned man with black hair and a broken
nose. He wasn't nervous but he wasn't at ease. We introduced ourselves and told him that we were enquiring in to a
series of murders.

'Is this about Major Carmichael?' he immediately asked.

'It might be connected,' I said.

'I was interviewed by Sergeant Billinghurst about that and
anyway, they found Jase – I mean Sergeant Phillips – guilty
of his murder.'

'Do you know Sergeant Billinghurst has been murdered?'

'No, sir.' His expression indicated he was clearly
surprised.

'What made you ask if it was about Major Carmichael?'

'I don't know really.'

'Is Corporal Hibberd implicated?' intervened the major.

Kitty took over. 'We don't think so, but we need background information on a number of people, so we're
hoping the corporal can fill in some blanks.'

'But I told the sergeant everything I saw,' said Hibberd.

'Yes, we know. As I said, this is part of a much wider
enquiry. We need lots of background information and you
may just be able to help us.'

He looked at Major Carter, perhaps for guidance, and
received a wry face and open hands, indicating that it was
up to him.

'Okay,' he said.

'Gil – can I call you Gil?'

'Yes, ma'am.'

'Thank you, Gil. You went to Washington with Jase Phillips. Please tell us why.'

He looked surprised. 'To see my sister.'

'Your sister?'

'Well, Jase was going to see her and he asked me to go
with him.'

Now it was Kitty's turn to look surprised. 'Let me see if I've got this right. Jase was married to your sister?'

'Yeah. They've got a couple of kids and she went off to America. Jase wanted them back and he thought I might be able to help, so I went with him.'

I was confused. Chief Inspector Wilkes had told me that Jase was married to *his* sister. 'Gil, I thought that Jase was married to Josephine Wilkes as was.'

'Yes, he was. He divorced my sister to marry her.'

Kitty looked at me, so I said, 'Tell me about your relationship with Jase. When did you first meet him?'

'Christ, sir, that was a long time ago: Jase was in a home and went to the same school as me, Nathfield Comprehensive. I was in year ten when he came. He was different and made an impression and fast. He was selected for the football team and the girls just followed him about. He played midfield and I was a central defender. We got on okay. Well, he got on okay with everybody, particularly the girls. He was in the county schools swimming team so he would go training in the morning and then come to school and then he would go swimming a couple of evenings a week and what with the football as well I'm surprised he'd time for the girls, but he did.' He laughed. 'Yes, he did a lot of them.'

'He did a lot of them? Please explain, Gil,' said Kitty.

'Well, you know.'

'I don't know,' she said.

'Well, it started with a couple of them who were in year eleven. One of them, Susan Hetherington, her dad was kinda rich. They had a big house and, well, they were away and she and her mate, Nadine Dalton – she was also rich – took him to her house and got him to shag them. That's when it started. They told the others in year eleven and it was a sort of girls' initiation to be shagged by Jase. What with the swimming and the football and the shagging, I'm surprised he wasn't bloody exhausted.'

60

'He, um, "did" a lot of girls then?' said Kitty.

'It was like he was a sort of pop idol. They'd go to the football and cheer him and to the swimming and support him.'

'And he "did" your sister?'

'No, not at school. That was after we joined up.'

'Tell me about Malcolm Wright. He was at the same school.'

'Yes, he was the year ahead of us. He was different then. He was in the home as well. The three of us sort of knocked about with each other at school. Malc was great then. He had a few girls as well but he had to work at it. Not like Jase.'

'What about you?'

'Me? I wasn't much good with the girls. I had a few but that was because I was a mate of Jase and they wanted introductions. So it wasn't me but I wasn't complaining.'

I intervened. 'When did the shaving start?' I was just flying a kite, following a hunch.

'That was the girls' gang really. It was a sort of agreed among the girls that if Jase had shagged them they'd shave off their, you know, pubic hair and that. Mind you, lots of the girls did it even though they hadn't, you know.'

I wondered how he knew but it was best not to ask.

'Did the other boys know this?'

'Yeah, I reckon everybody in the school knew, even the teachers. Jase even had one of them.'

'He was a real Lothario then,' said Kitty

'I dunno what that is.'

'A ladies' man.'

'Christ, no! He didn't do nothin' to attract women, like dress up and the like. In fact I think that there were only two women he was ever really interested in.'

'They were?' I asked.

'My sister and Gabriel Holt's sister. And that's what caused the break up.'

61

'Explain please.'

'He was married to my sister and he met Gabriel's sister. My sister saw them together and – wham – she just took off. I don't know why, though. She knew other women just couldn't stay away from him.'

I was really confused now. 'When did Josephine come on the scene?'

'Oh, that was later.'

'After he'd broken up with your sister.'

'I suppose so. Yes, it must have been.'

'So what about Gabriel Holt's sister?'

'Well, they were still friends. I'm not sure it was, you know, but Jase really liked her.'

'Christ, he certainly got around,' said Kitty, looking at me and smiling. I had an idea what she was thinking. I had to get back on track.

'In the army, did the other soldiers know about him being shaved down?'

'Hold on!' exclaimed Kitty. 'This woman thing. He had intercourse with a large number of girls at school. He then had multiple relationships in the army. He married your sister but wasn't faithful.' Kitty paused looking at Gil.

He nodded.

'He was seeing Gabriel Holt's sister and that created a breakup with your sister and then he married Rod Wilkes' sister. Now he has a relationship with Celia Foley and she is AWOL.'

Gil nodded.

'But there were lots of other relationships?'

'Yes ma'am.'

'Did this create problems with other men?'

'Sometimes.'

'Any really serious?'

'Well, he was cited in a couple of divorces.'

'Anybody who really hated Phillips?'

'Well, I suppose so.'

'Anybody in particular?'

'I don't think so, well, Wrighty was pissed off by Jase, he was jealous.'

'You said Malcolm Wright changed.'

'Yes. Jase and I joined the Army Foundation College and Malc joined directly, 'cos he was older than us.'

'What's the foundation college?' asked Kitty.

'Well, it's like what used to be called the Junior Leaders. You can join up when you're over sixteen but too young to join the army. They train you as a soldier and complete your education, sort of.'

'Thanks. You were telling us about Malcolm Wright,' I said.

'Yes, well, he'd always been in trouble at school but it was nothing serious. Well, we didn't think so, although the police gave him a couple of warnings and he saw a magistrate once. But after he was in the army he got up to all sorts of stuff – smuggling and drugs and porn, all sorts of stuff. Then the major got hold of him and he settled down. I reckon Jase got the major to have a word with him.'

'The major was?'

'Major Carmichael. Well, he was a captain then.'

'Go on.'

'He made lance corporal but got busted and then the major had him as a sort of communications specialist in the company.'

'Let me go back to Jase. In the army, what did he do apart from girls?' I asked.

'Before you go on to Jase, Wrighty had a social worker at school,' said Gil.

'Why?'

'Don't know really. She came to see him a lot.'

'Do you know her name?' Kitty asked.

'Yes, um, Miss Perkins.'

Kitty was making notes. 'Well remembered.'

'Yer, well, one of the girls was seeing her as well and there was this old song, "Pretty Polly Perkins from Paddington Green" and she used to sing it when Miss Perkins came to the school. Kind of a joke really.'

I picked up the questioning again. 'About Jase: what did he do apart from girls?'

'Funny that; he was always busy. He did some sport but not seriously like at school. He started knocking around with Malc a bit and the major. That was another thing. The major had a lot of respect for Jase. Sometimes you'd think that Jase was the major and Toffee was the sergeant.'

'Toffee?'

'Yeah, that's what we called him. He was a real Rupert.' He turned to Major Carter. 'Sorry, sir.' Then he turned back to us. 'A toff, so we called him Toffee. Not to his face, like, because he could be a right bastard sometimes, so he wasn't a toff really, sort of a toff that wasn't one, so we called him Toffee. He had this hero reputation but it was Captain Gillen and Lieutenant Mortlake that carried him in Iraq, and Jase of course. Jase was the best soldier in the company. He should have been at least a captain.'

'What about Gabriel Holt?'

'I don't want to answer that.'

'Why not?'

'Look, there are some things better not talked about.'

'Is that because of Gabriel's sexuality?'

'Look, everybody liked Gabriel. He was a good soldier, brave as they come. He was the sort of guy you want beside you in a tough situation. But he was, well... I don't wanna talk about it.'

'Okay, just one question; what was his relationship with Major Carmichael?'

'That's enough,' said Major Carter. 'Major Carmichael is not here to defend himself.' I was puzzled by the intervention. So Gabriel was gay, why the intervention?

64

I chipped in. 'Let me put this bluntly, Major. We're looking into at least six murders. There seems to be connections to drugs and definite links to organised crime so quite frankly we don't give a shit about someone who is dead and looks like he's at the heart of the killings and the drugs. We need to build a background picture and that's what we're going to do.'

'I think it's time we left.'

'Then leave, Major, and we'll take your boyo into custody, charged with obstruction. We just want background and we'll get it.'

13

There was a strained silence. The major had a decision to make. Gil broke the impasse.

'He was like you, you know.' He was looking at me.

'Who was like me?'

'Jase was like you.'

'Tell us,' said Kitty.

'He was tough and direct like the captain here. He didn't suffer fools gladly or anybody who got uppity. I watched the captain when he was investigating the major's killing. The women just tried to get noticed by him. But that was where he was different from Jase; he didn't seem to notice or if he did notice didn't do nothin' about it.'

'So, Gil, you're observant when it comes to people. Out of ten, I'd like you to give us a score for the names I give you for the likelihood that they'd murder a woman. Will you do that?'

'This sounds like a macabre game show,' said the major.

Kitty ignored him. 'Okay, let's start with the captain here, just to set a baseline. Ten is extremely likely and one extremely unlikely.'

I must admit I'd never heard of such an approach used by police before, but it did seem to have links with Kelly's Personal Construct Theory.

'The captain, I'd give him four,' said Gil.

'Based on what?'

'Well, he's tough enough to do it and I reckon cold-blooded enough not to worry about it. No, make that a

66

three 'cos he has this human streak and he'd need one hell of a good reason, but given the reason he'd not even think about it. No take that back to four.'

'Okay, what about Gabriel?'

'No way! I'd give him a one. He'd only kill a woman to put her out of her misery.'

'What about the major?'

'Now you're talking. I'd give him an eight, no nine. You're going to ask me why. He didn't like women. I'd say he hated them but he used to hide it and be courteous and all that shit, but he could kill them. He had this ruthless, killing streak. I saw him shoot four Iraqis who were running away, two of them were women. We knew they weren't terrorists and weren't even armed. He just killed them for fun because he could. No, definitely a nine.'

'Now look here–' the major attempted an interruption.

'Shut the fuck up, Major, or you're out of here.'

He looked at me and shook his head.

Kitty went on. 'Any other reason he might kill women? You gave him a score of nine.'

'Yes, he was a show-off. He'd do it in front of others just to look the "big I am", but only if he could get away with it.'

'So does that reduce the nine?'

'No, that keeps it being a nine or even a ten. If things went wrong he was never to blame. It was always some other poor bastard.'

'What about Malc?'

'I'd give him a nine, only because he'd be shit scared of being caught. Otherwise I'd give him a ten.'

'Why?'

'Well he became a real nasty bastard. He didn't give a shit about killing anything or anybody. He'd absolutely no conscience. If he had to kill one of us so he could get out of trouble, he'd do it. He became a coward, but I reckon that was the drugs.'

'He was on drugs?'

'Yeah, he was shooting smack.'

'Anything particular about women?'

'I'm not sure, but as I said, he was jealous of Jase, and I think he hated the fact that Jase got all the pussy he could handle and he couldn't get it unless he paid for it or took it.'

'Took it?'

'Look, I can't prove this but the rumour was he raped at least three Iraqi women.'

'What about a score for Jase then?'

'Maximum two.'

'Why two?'

'Like Gabriel, to put them out of their misery or in self-defence.'

'So Gabriel wouldn't kill a woman in self-defence?'

'No, in a battle he would, but it isn't a woman then it's an enemy soldier.'

'What about you then, Gil?'

'Me. Only my bloody wife if she doesn't stop shagging the guy down the fuckin' road.'

'Oh, I'm sorry I asked,' said Kitty.

'No, she'll get over it when I get home, so she's quite safe really.' He gave a wry smile. 'I'm not sure how safe his balls are though.'

'I'd like to ask you a couple of questions about Jase, about the girls at school and the fact that women were attracted to him.'

Gil nodded.

'Think back a couple of years. Can you remember the names of any women he slept with?'

'Christ, Captain.' He thought. 'Well, in Iraq there was Maali Mizher and Ghadah Qasim. In Afghanistan there was a woman named Uzuri I think. There was an RAF officer but I can't remember her name.'

'Susan Thomas?'

'Yeah, that's her, a flight lieutenant.'

'Thank you, Gil. You've been a real assistance to us. Any questions you want to ask us?'

'Only one. What happened with Sergeant Billinghurst?'

Kitty looked at me.

'She was shot but the bastard who shot her is now dead.'

'Good. I mean I'm glad he's dead. I liked her. She was real professional and fair.'

'Thank you, Gil, you have been a real help in clarifying some things that have been bothering us. And can we thank you, Major, for you forbearance? Not easy when a fellow officer is being investigated.'

We shook hands with both the men and left. If image was anything to go by we had two suspects clearly in the frame but the only thing that counts is evidence.

14

We set off for home mid morning. The road was quiet but Kitty's car wasn't. It sounded lumpy. I hadn't noticed that as we drove down.

'Problem, Kitty?'

'Seems like it. Better drop into a garage.'

Just then her car surrendered. It didn't just conk out; it slowly lost speed, the engine rattled and the exhaust farted. Kitty pulled over and we sat there at the side of the road listening to the lumpy engine.

'You'd best switch it off,' I said.

'I bloody have,' she snapped.

'Oh.' I decided to stay silent and then decided to speak. 'Shall I have a look?'

'Do you know anything about cars?'

'Well, no, but I can see if something's fallen off.'

The contempt on her face was tangible. Then a Merc pulled up gently and almost silently past us and stopped. A man emerged from the passenger side and walked back to us. He was a big man and tapped on my window. I smiled at him. Well, smiling seemed my only option as he had opened his jacket and a holstered weapon could be seen under his left arm.

'Stay here,' I told Kitty and got out of the car before she had the chance to argue, let alone think of following. The man nodded towards the Merc and I watched as the driver got out and opened the rear door. With my arms half-raised in submission, I got in and sat beside a woman who was older than me, but that's not difficult or even surprising. What was surprising was her necklace. I didn't know anything about jewellery but I would bet that necklace cost a bomb and it was matched by the rings on her left hand, an engagement ring, a wedding ring and an eternity ring, and earrings. She was probably late thirties or early forties and was a walking invitation for a mugging. Not that anyone would take on the two heavies with her. She was very slender, not skinny though, with pale skin, fine skin, almost luminous, and dark shiny hair, expensively dressed in black, which set off the diamonds. I had seen her before but had no idea where or when. Where on earth would somebody dressed like that be going at this time of the day?

She looked at me assessing me. 'You are Robinson?' Her voice indicated she was not impressed with what she had observed.

'Yes, and you are?'

Ignoring me she looked out of the window. She was waiting for somebody but it was somebody she didn't know, she just had that sort of tension about her.

'Are we waiting for somebody?' I asked.

She put the index finger of her right hand to her lips (it's amazing how I can observe and remember things when I'm tense) and then a Land Rover pulled up.

'I think you'd better get out, Mr Robinson,' she said. She was so polite and at the same time dismissive. I obeyed. Her two heavies then got back in the Merc and her window went down. She spoke to a heavy from the Land Rover; another heavy was now with him. 'Persuade Mr Robinson that he should take a holiday.'

'What about the copper, my lady?'

My lady? She had to be one of The Family.

'No, she can take him to hospital.'

The Merc pulled away, quietly and powerfully.

71

'You Robinson?'

'Yes.'

'Heard about you.'

'Nothing good I hope.'

'No, just enough to want to kick the shit out of you. The message is simple. You will forget all about a certain major having anything to do with any killing of any women at any time. Should this not happen, there will be consequences.'

'Oh I see. Can I go now?'

He smiled. He had some broken teeth. He was a tall guy, around six two, broad shoulders, thick neck, probably worked out with weights as his arms were muscular, bulky. His black hair was long and not well kept but thick. He was probably under thirty and tough. It showed on his face with thick eyebrows, high cheekbones and a broken nose. He stepped forward, in range. Silly mistake. Before he could gather any form of attack my right fist hit his Adam's apple. He was gasping for breath and making a gurgling sound as I caught his jacket and my forehead hit his nose hard. Well, it hurt me. I then thrust him back and he went down. I kicked him in the area that causes considerable pain to the male of the species then kicked his head. That sent him to sleep. The second man was cautious. He had a knife, blade open, and he was backing away.

'You best run, son, because when I've finished with you, you won't be able to walk let alone run.' I walked towards him. Slowly, he continued to back away, but wasn't looking where he was going because he fell backwards into a ditch. It was half-filled with muddy water that closed around his waist with him sitting on the bottom. I picked up a stick and poked him.

'Who sent you?'

He shook his head.

'You want to drown?' I poked him again. 'Who?'

'Jake, stop.' It was Kitty. My stick slashed his face.

'He will get you, you bastard.'

'Who will?' My stick hit him again.

'His fucking Lordship, that's who.'

'No, he didn't send you. The woman did. Who is she?'

Silence. The stick swished through the air just past the tip of his nose.

'Lady Bethany.'

'Thank you.' I looked at Kitty.

'Does he mean?' She paused. 'Rupert Carmichael's daughter.'

'I think he does. The major's sister. Can you drive a Land Rover?'

'Yes, but I'll have to report this,' she said.

'No, I don't think so. It'll just get lost in the noise of real crime.'

She knew I was right but she didn't like it.

'So, let's tow your car to a garage,' I suggested and we did, leaving our less than friendly attackers at the side of the road.

15

When we finally arrived at Kitty's office we went over the information we had. Some of it had to be good but it was difficult to build a clear picture. That picture, however, had three definite names – Carmichael, Wright and Holt. They had to be our focus. As we were agreeing on this, my phone rang. It was Sam. She had a message. The top man himself wanting to see me – Rupert Carmichael, Earl of Charnforth. Now, that was a turn up, but not a surprise really. The only problem was whether I would walk away from the meeting or be carried out and dumped somewhere. Ah, well, I'd stick my neck out and hope my head didn't get chopped off.

Kitty wanted me to wear a wire, but I thought that was too risky as I would probably be searched and maybe scanned. I rang Barrow. He was uncomfortable and suggested I leave my mobile switched on and he would have it tracked. Once more I was going into the unknown, but I did have a mobile phone fully charged and ready for action. I laughed at myself.

It had been a grey day threatening rain. I suppose that matched my mood, waiting to enter the lion's den. Now, with the late evening, the rain had started. I stood by the Berkeley on Wilton Place, on the corner, where I'd been told to wait, with the five storeys of light brown stone and windows rising behind me. I must admit to being nervous. I was unarmed; well, I had a phone – wow! I remember some history thing, George VI, that Sam had been reading. The King said, 'Give me a light that I may tread safely into the unknown.' And the man said, 'Go out into the darkness and put your hand into the hand of God.' That was a fat lot of use as I'm an atheist armed with a mobile phone. Still, it had a built-in torch.

After a few minutes of waiting, a taxi rolled up, a standard London black cab. It stopped opposite me with the window down. The driver leaned across.

'Jake Robinson?'

'Yep.'

'Hop in please, sir.'

I climbed in the back. 'Where are we going?'

'Now that's a bit of a problem, sir. I'm waiting to be told but I've been given a general direction.'

I sat back and waited in the hands of a taxi driver as he pulled smoothly away. The cab radio cackled. How these drivers understood the voice in the static was beyond me.

'We've a destination, sir.'

'Where?'

'Hamilton Street.'

'Did you say Hamilton Street?'

I knew better than to ask but I assumed the phone tracking would be insufficient. Now whoever was listening to my phone had, at least, part of an address. By knowing the destination I was strangely comforted. More than that, I was relaxed, well, relaxing. The taxi was weaving through a number of back doubles and I'd absolutely no idea where we were or the direction we were going in. I'd a feeling we were going north and east. Eventually, we pulled over next to a seedy-looking club in a street of small shops, a bookie, an Indian takeaway, a sex shop and a newsagent. The club name, in a flickering blue neon strip light, was Blue Heaven. It had to be a strip club with a name like that in blue neon. Two large bouncers were on the door with a girl with a very large bust with only her nipples covered, a diamond in her navel and long legs that went right up to her bum and down again. The only thing you couldn't see was where they came together at the top. It was too cold to be dressed like that; well, it was in the dark at night.

'There you go, sir. I'll pick you up when you leave.'

'The Blue Heaven is my destination then, driver?'

'I reckon so, sir.'

Strangely, I found it immensely reassuring that the driver thought I was going to leave and he would pick me up and the bonus was my trackers now had an address. I turned my phone off, climbed out of the cab and, as the door clicked shut, the taxi pulled away. One of the bouncers opened the door to the club.

'Good evening, sir. Please follow Neaira.'

It seemed I was expected. For some reason that I didn't understand the name Neaira registered with me. Her hips swayed provocatively as I followed her down the dimly lit passageway. Then I remembered; Neaira was the name of a courtesan of Ancient Greece. How appropriate, perhaps this woman had read some classics.

She stopped in front of a green door. It was odd. It was covered in baize, like a snooker table. A tune was in my head: 'Green door, what's that secret you're keeping?' It was a pop singer named Frankie Vaughan asking the question. Then I remembered it was from a 1950s record my grand-mother had. Neaira knocked three times and the door opened, but nobody 'laughed out loud' as it said in the song. She stepped aside for me to enter but not quite far enough. Her bust gently brushed my upper arm as I entered. I wondered if she practised that.

The room was large and the earl was sitting at a polished dining table in the centre of the room using a mobile phone. Two places were laid and he was seated at the one facing me. The lights were low and brighter over the table.

There was music playing; it wasn't 'Green Door' but some gentle, sophisticated, classical piece.

'Please sit down, Jake.' He remained seated. 'Would you like a drink before we eat?'

A waiter appeared next to me and the earl returned to his mobile phone.

'Sir?' asked the waiter.

'G and T, please.'

'Bombay Sapphire or Tanqueray number ten, sir?'

'Tanqueray sounds good to me. Thank you.'

'Ice and lemon, sir?'

'Yes, thank you.'

This was way over the top in terms of service or seemed to be in these surroundings. My drink, at least a double, arrived in a crystal tumbler in what seemed only seconds. A second crystal tumbler containing a pale amber liquid was placed within reach of the earl. He was drinking double whisky or brandy. I poured the tonic water into my tumbler and the ice bounced about. It was at times like these that I was pleased about my upbringing, polished by the army's knife and fork course.

The earl eventually rang off and switched off his phone. For the first time I was able to observe my host. I assumed that he was my host. He may of course have been my captor or numerous other things. I knew one or two things about him; he was Rupert Carmichael, Earl of Charnforth and Major Michael Carmichael's father. Most importantly, he was the head of The Family, the top man. In America he would be the Godfather, *Il capo dei capi*, and I suppose that was how he struck me: clearly a man of power and confidence. He was large. Even though he was sitting he seemed well over 6 foot and probably weighed 18 stone. Although he was large I had the impression he wasn't overweight. I supposed he was in his early sixties although he didn't look that old. The full head of dark hair made him look younger. I wondered if it was dyed – maybe that Grecian 2000 stuff or whatever it was called. If that was the case, was he a vain man?

'Thank you for agreeing to see me. I thought a meal together might enable us to get to know each other.' He tipped his head to one side. 'I apologise for the mis-understanding the other day. I should have listened to what I had been told.'

His voice and accent were as expected: deep, smooth and well paced with impeccable upper-class pronunciation. No falsification of the accent – it was smooth, old-fashioned BBC English. But I had an odd feeling that the whole epi-sode wasn't real. It seemed like a scene from *The Godfather*. All it needed was a *consigliare* in attendance.

'Do you dine here often, sir?' I assumed 'sir' as the mode of address as I think I might find 'your grace' a step too far.

'Please call me Rupert,' he paused. 'Unfortunately not often enough. The food is magnificent and the individual post-dinner relaxation has always proved to be most stimu-lating and enjoyable.'

I wondered what that might be. I could guess if Neaira was anything to go by.

'I thought we'd start with some prawns.'

As he spoke they arrived and looked magnificent. They sat in a bed of watercress and at the side of them were a dip and a plate of brown bread triangles. With the prawns arrived a pair of crystal wine glasses and a bottle of white wine. The wine waiter showed me the bottle and said, 'The chef recommends a white wine that he's just acquired. It's a Cortese di Gavi. Would you like to try it, sir?'

He was addressing me but the earl responded. 'I'm sure it'll be delightful but if I remember rightly the captain prefers his white wine chilled a few degrees more than the forty-eight degrees Fahrenheit that is usual for Italian wines, so this is at forty-six degrees.'

'Yes, your grace,' said the wine waiter.

How the hell did he know that? I was no wine buff but I did like white wine well chilled and I knew the Bel Vedere did chill it a bit more for me because I once mentioned that their wine was not properly chilled, or was that Sam? Perhaps I'd been remembered when Sam and I went to the Bel Vedere. No, that was far too fanciful. If I recall, it was warm. I liked this wine and it was not expensive. Conclusion: they'd done considerable homework on me. The fact that I had been tracked with both Kitty and Sam registered.

'Thank you, Rupert. What is it you want to know if we're to get to know each other?'

'Yes, I was told you were direct. I think we've had some misunderstandings and it would be good if we put them behind us.'

I tried a prawn and nibbled at a triangle of the thinly cut brown bread.

'I understand you met my daughter Bethany the other day.'

'Yes, Rupert.'

'She was inordinately fond of Michael you know. I do apologise for any inconvenience she may have caused.'

'Apology accepted, Rupert.'

'Thank you, Jake.' It was an odd formality. He was weighing me up but I couldn't read what he was thinking. 'I expect she was dressed up like her mother.' It fell in to place; she wasn't going anywhere, she was being somebody. Are all these old families crackers? I shrugged. What can you say?

'My son, Michael, was a disappointment to me.' He stopped and stared at me. He clearly saw the disbelief on my face. 'I surprise you, Jake.'

'Well, I must admit that you do.'

'He was a bloody pansy.' Now this was a shock. This handsome hero was a homosexual? This wasn't even on our radar. We had an idea that he didn't like women but that could have been male arrogance or misogyny. Now the intervention of the major when we interviewed Gil Hibberd made sense. Carmichael's fellow officers knew he was gay. 'I even employed two young men at the house when he was a boy because they were. . .shirt-lifters I think you call them, to keep him out of trouble with the local boys and avoid him catching some incurable illness. At school, Antony, Michael's cousin kept him out of any serious trouble in the sexual arena. Lucky really. Michael was in love with Antony. Always had been since they were about eight, although Antony was quite normal.'

'Quite normal?'

'Just a figure of speech. He started shagging gals when he was about thirteen. That gave us some problems. A couple of them quite costly, but by the time he was fifteen he was more mature and responsible. He could have gone on to great things if you hadn't killed him. No, don't deny it.'

'I wasn't going to.'

'Good for you, Jake. I don't quite understand why you did it but that's not what we're here to talk about. Like the prawns? Good. Like some more? No?'

He signalled to the waiter. I hadn't spoken and as far as I knew. I gave no signals but he was correct both times. I liked the prawns and I didn't want any more.

16

The waiter came over and cleared the table. He then said or rather announced, 'This evening, gentlemen, for your main course we have slow-cooked rump of Cornish lamb with parsnip and vanilla mash, glazed root vegetables and creamed savoy cabbage scented with thyme. We also have fresh mint sauce and freshly made English mustard if you wish.'

'Sounds magnificent,' I said. I then waited until the waiter left and said, 'I'm confused, sir – sorry, Rupert. Either you want to tell me something or you want me to tell you something and I'm not sure which way it is.'

'Yes, I just want you to have the full picture before I ask something of you.' He paused.

'Okay,' I said.

'My son was not only a pansy but also a prat. Bright enough, but he was not smart enough to rise to the top of The Family. He trailed behind his cousin, Antony, whom he loved, and his half-brother, Randolph, whom he resented. Yes, I know you know about Antony, Randolph, Beth and Annabelle. He wanted to prove himself worthy so he put his life on the line. He didn't even understand that I couldn't even use him as, as the Americans call them, a hitman. He was too reckless. Sooner or later, the army would see it. He wanted to show me he could run a business.'

The waiter came with the main course and we were silent, apart from thanking him as he served it and the whole rigmarole from silver serving dishes, until he left.

'As I was saying, he wanted to prove he could run a business. Well, he couldn't. The business was in reality run by Jason Phillips and a woman, Susan Thomas. They weren't really up to doing it part-time.' I had a double take. So Jase was running the Iraq drug business! Josey was right.

'That surprised you, Jake. Yes, Jason was a really good operator and he could have gone a long way in The Family, but it required full-time dedication and focus on the financial side. We put in people so that it didn't go belly up, Otis Brockett and Hashi Syedain.'

I registered the names and the 'we'. Rupert Carmichael instantly noticed.

'Aha, so you know the names, Jake.'

'I'd like a couple of items of information.'

'Okay, Jake.'

'When did you appoint Otis Brockett and Hashi Syedain?'

'Let me see, that must be about eighteen months ago.'

'It couldn't have been two years ago?'

'Definitely not. Michael went to Washington to talk about a job there. It was then.'

'But that was only six months ago.'

'Ah, yes, he went six months ago but he went earlier, then something blew up in Iraq – please excuse the pun – so his appointment was postponed.'

Otis Brockett and Hashi Syedain were in the frame as serial killers, now they were eliminated.

'You said "we" when Brockett and Syedain were appointed.'

He smiled and nodded. 'Yes, you're as good as I was told you were. No, I appointed them but not without advice. Hence, the "we".'

'So, you were saying that Michael was an incompetent businessman. Jase Phillips and Susan Thomas were carrying the business but they were not up to it or rather up to the financial aspects?'

'I'm probably being a little hard if that's the way you're interpreting what I said. Phillips and Thomas were good but they were part-time. They needed full-time support so I gave that to them.'

'So it was handling the money side of the business that was the weak area?'

'Yes, but how do you know?'

'Brockett and Syedain are, I think, money men working for Charnforth Wealth Management or Whitehaven Investments.'

He looked at me for a long time. 'You really do know a lot about The Family don't you, Jake?'

'We do our best, Rupert.'

He nodded. He was making a decision and I hoped it wasn't to kill me.

'Negotiating the logistics of getting raw material out and processing it was being handled well. How to pay requires a different set of skills in this international trade and was likely to lead to exposures.'

'I'd like to ask another question, please, Rupert.'

'And I know what it is. Why did I have your sergeant killed and try to have you assassinated?'

He was much more upfront than I thought he would be. I just waited.

'I was hearing rumours that Michael was being accused of murder. It appeared that somebody close to my son, Randolph, had gathered some information. I know he didn't do the killings but it seemed that you and your sergeant had the basis of a case. So I acted, more in haste than in logic. I rarely act emotionally but I had to protect my son. I realised later that you were not hell bent on exposing my son for these crimes, and the person in question was unreliable.'

'But you still wanted to distract me from Michael.'

'Yes, I was still not sure about you. I decided dissuasion

might be a useful tactic. I should have known better after the prison episodes.'

It seemed to me that Rupert knew more than me about the serial killings.

'What about Jason Phillips?'

'Ah, yes! I had mixed motives there. He was the one who put your sergeant on to Michael. He also killed Michael. He was where he should be for his crime but, well, family is family.'

'So you don't think Michael was a serial killer?'

He looked at me for a long time. 'My son was a lot of things, Jake, including brave, stupid and a homosexual, but he was not a serial killer.' He said this as a challenge, almost as if to say, if you prove otherwise I'll kill you. I was struggling with his assessment of his son. Nobody gets to be a major in the British Army, let alone a lieutenant colonel, unless they are very bright.

'You had Jase Phillips killed because he was likely to pin the murders on to Michael?'

'Yes. I know I was wrong. It was stupid and I rarely do stupid things but my emotions distorted my thinking and it was only when you went into the prison that I saw things more clearly. I had to admire your bravery. Policemen are not popular with cat-A prisoners.'

'I was well protected.'

'So I heard and you killed some people, although I feel what you were likely to be subjected to was not something I'd sanction. Tell me, what did you think of Peter Jackson?'

'Um, how can I say this? He was not fully on board.'

'I think you've just confirmed something that I suspected. Thank you.'

'So what is it you want of me, Rupert?'

'Jake, oh, Jake, if only you'd been my son. You don't piss about do you? You just go straight for the jugular. I like that. I really admire that. What do I want of you? Now you've confronted me I have to think clearly. Let me start at the beginning then.' He stopped and was looking down into his lap. I could feel the logic ticking over but there was also a lot of emotion there. 'I want you to prove beyond a shadow of a doubt who the serial killer is or was. If it was my son, you're going to have to convince me. If you accuse him, and you can't convince me, I'll have you killed. If you can convince me you live.'

'And if I can't find out who the serial killer is?'

'Then, my fine friend, we face a dilemma, but I'm a good judge of character and ability. I know, I just know, you'll solve this case.'

'Your son, Randolph, has offered me fifty grand to find out who killed Jason Phillips. I knew who actually did the killing and I killed him. I also now know who ordered it. Do I tell him?'

'No, I'll tell him and you'll get your fifty grand. I'd also like to thank you for killing Ratty. Yes, that must be worth an extra fifty grand. He was on the verge of being a problem. He'd started on heroin and hinted at blackmail. Now for pudding, it's something I love.'

Killing and pudding were on about the same level of importance for Rupert Carmichael, Earl of Charnforth. No, perhaps pudding was more important.

'It's bread and butter pudding with custard. How does that suit you, Jake?'

'You really have done your homework on me haven't you, Rupert?'

'Oh, you noticed.' He raised his right hand with just the index finger uncurled. His wrist didn't leave the table edge, but the waiter went into action. Now that was power.

'Have you any view as to who the killer is?' I asked

'Yes, but I want the job done properly and seen to be done properly.' He was thinking. He then focused again on me, nodded and smiled to himself. He'd either made a decision or he was pleased with a decision he'd made. 'Do you read the *Kensington, Chelsea and Westminster Gazette*?'

'I'm afraid not.'

'Nice little weekly read. It has a number of titbits in it that are interesting to residents of that area. You do live there, don't you?'

'Um, yes.' I wondered where this was going.

He reached down onto the chair next to him. 'Oh, read this in obituaries.'

I read the marked entry:

Mr Charles McIvor-Johnstone, Son of Sir Arthur McIvor-Johnstone, the owner and operator of the McIvor Estates in the Highlands of Scotland and the Johnstone Brewers and Distillers companies, was found dead in his apartment on Wednesday. The circumstances of his death are not clear but foul play is not suspected. Succession will now pass to his sister, Claris. This will be the first time the family business will be headed by a woman. Charles, who was progressing rapidly in the civil service, gained a first-class honours degree in economics at Cambridge and an MBA at Harvard University in North America.

'Coffee, Jake?'

'No, thank you, Rupert.'

'What do you think?'

'I don't think he'll be talking to anybody about much.'

'True, very true.' He smiled and nodded.

'I've arranged some private, after-dinner entertainment if you wish it.'

'Thank you, but no thank you, Rupert.'

'I knew you'd say that, but I think the young lady will be disappointed.'

We walked to the door of the club. The few people in the passageway flattened themselves against the walls to allow us to pass. Rupert didn't even seem to notice them. We shook hands at the door of the club and he bid me goodnight as the taxi pulled up quietly.

'Jake,' he said. It was almost an afterthought. 'If you ever want a job you can ask your own payment and I'll employ you.'

'Thank you, Rupert.' I could almost describe the job he would offer me, either *consigliare* or a *caporegime*.

I thought about his entertainment offer. She may have been disappointed but Rupert Carmichael, Earl of Charnforth, wouldn't have any compromising photos of me and any leaks that might have come from Charles were now irrevocably blocked. I also knew he offered me a job because I turned down the entertainment offer. Morality is different for these people.

The taxi was taking me home so I relaxed in the back and thought. I was now convinced that Michael Carmichael was not the serial killer. Kitty may not have been but I was. He disliked women so was unlikely to get into any relationship with them. He was homosexual so the rape and oral sex would be unlikely. The beatings were definitely possible. Could he have been associated with the killings? Yes, it was possible but extremely unlikely.

17

I got back home to find Sam waiting.

'They released you from protective custody then,' I said.

'Oh, I couldn't cope with it. I sent Ethel home so I'm a free agent again. Give me a cuddle.' She was warm and soft and lifted my very soul. We collapsed onto the settee and watched a recording of some drivel on TV about a bunch of inarticulate and miserable individuals who lived, apparently, in the east end of London. Sam seemed to relate to it so I stayed schtum but I couldn't see any jokes or much of a story, it was just sad.

Much later, she said, 'There was a message on your phone. It was a Miss Perkins. Somebody has contacted her. Who is Miss Perkins?'

'She is a passionate spinster who has a thing for MI5 officers.'

'Oh. Piss off Robinson.'

'It must have been Kitty. Setting me up for a hot date.'

'If you don't want to tell me that's okay. You can sleep in the spare room.'

'No, no, not the spare room, in the dark, I'll be frightened. Okay, okay, I surrender. I'll tell you. Miss Pretty Polly Perkins from Paddington Green is a social worker and one of our suspects was a client of hers when he was at school.'

'Okay so she *is* a hot date. I forgive you Jake Robinson.'

The next morning, I phoned Miss Perkins and arranged to see her. We met in a social services office that was total chaos. There were files everywhere and the ringing phones were unanswered. You could see she was stressed. Her hair was stringy, she had black rings around her eyes and bags under them and her skin was pallid. She was skinny so clearly wasn't eating properly. She made nervous jerky movements and this was not to do with talking to me, although my presence wouldn't have helped. This was long-term environmental stress, probably due to the sort of work she was involved with.

I suggested we went to a coffee shop on the same road as her offices and she agreed. It was quiet, with just a dozen plastic-topped tables and only three were occupied. With a coffee each and a packet of mixed biscuits we sat down. She was totally focused on her coffee, stirring it slowly.

'I'd like you to tell me about Malcolm Wright,' I said.

She looked at me from under her eyebrows without raising her head. Her pale, drawn face showed concern. Fear? Perhaps.

'I'm not sure what I'm allowed to tell you.' There was deep worry here. It seemed personal but I didn't know why. Perhaps it would come out.

'That's okay. If you don't want to tell me anything now it's okay. We don't need your information at the moment but if we do need it we'll take the necessary action to get it.'

'Why?' So more than one thing about Wright concerned her.

'We're conducting an investigation in to some murders; Malcolm Wright's name has come up a number of times. We need some background and your name came up.'

She looked at me for a long time and was thinking. There seemed to be some relief. How could murder be less worrying than some other investigation? She pinched her lips together and stared at her coffee, probably weighing up the effect of what she might tell me or of not telling me. A tick started on the left side of her mouth. I had concerns. She needed help. At minimum a holiday would be good. Say nothing, Jake.

'He had a rough childhood you know.' She still stared at her coffee cup. I waited. 'He didn't stand a chance.' She was talking to her coffee or herself. She didn't seem to be talking to me. Was this a defence mechanism?

'Would you like to tell me about it?'

She looked up. We made eye contact then she looked away and back again. She sighed and bit her bottom lip with tears in her eyes then shook her head, looked down and spoke softly. 'In the home, Attlee House, he was beaten for wetting the bed. He was very young, perhaps five, maybe six at that time. He went home to his mother and then he was taken back into care. I'm not sure why. This ill treatment started again when he was fostered. His foster father was physically brutal, punishing him severely for any infraction of the house rules. Malcolm didn't complain. It was the norm for him. If he didn't finish a meal, he got it at the next mealtime. In fact, it was left on the table and he wasn't allowed to touch it until the next mealtime. He was eventually taken back into care and he'd only eat certain things, the things he had in the foster home, like baked beans, bread and jam. He'd just go hungry if those foods weren't available.' She stopped and looked at me.

'Go on. I'm listening.' I nodded. I'd met the restricted diet thing a number of times in the army. She needed the reassurance that I was making no judgements.

'It was reported by other boys that he ill-treated animals. It was believed he'd killed the cat of a neighbour who reported him for being a nuisance. He was also blamed for draining the school pond so that the fish died, although this was never proved. This cruelty seemed to stop when he went to secondary school. It may have been because he was fostered again. He once told me that his foster mother had sexual relations with him if he behaved himself so he behaved himself. I didn't report it because he seemed settled.'

'Seems like it was a good plan to me,' I said.

She smiled, relieved, looking inwards. She knew I was joking and smiled at the idea that all boys would behave themselves with this reinforcement.

'He was seen as a bit of an odd ball at school but he was never bullied nor was he a bully. He was meticulously clean and his schoolbooks and clothes were immaculate. I understand that this all changed when he joined the army. The exact opposite of what might be expected.'

'It might be that the incentive to behave himself had changed,' I said.

Miss Perkins nodded. There was something else. It was one of those policeman things; you just know. She picked up her cup and swirled round the dregs.

'Would you like another cup?'

'Oh, no thank you.'

She played with the spoon. She was considering what she might tell me. I stayed quiet.

'He came home on leave after he'd been in the army about three or four months. He came to see me. We had sex. He said it was to thank me for being his social worker.' She started to cry. I waited and eventually the tears subsided. 'I'm sorry. I must go.' She grabbed her handbag as she left, but stopped at the door and turned back to me. She took a deep breath and said, 'I've a son.'

I had a horrible sinking feeling.

'*His* son and he's beautiful.'

'Wait, does Wright know?'

'No, he mustn't know.'

She ran out of the shop and disappeared along the road. I understood her initial fear now. No, Wright mustn't know, and the boy mustn't know who his father is. I had another cup of coffee and thought it all over. Here were all the

91

symptoms of someone with a background that could lead to some form of sociopathic behaviour. He had to be in the frame and I'll ensure Miss Perkins won't be within a million miles of it nor will her son.

18

My mobile rang. It was Kitty.

'Jake, we think we've found Celia.'

I could tell from her voice that this was not good news.

'She's dead then.' Oh, Jake, you wanker, you should have stayed schtum.

'Come to the police station in Heartlybridge in Devon. The superintendent at Exeter said the locals will brief us and then we can see the scene.' She was direct, and to the point. I could hear the angst in her voice. Why us? was the question in my head, but I didn't ask it.

'Where are you now?'

'I'm on my way to pick up Gaygan. We should be there about two.'

I returned to the flat and discovered Sam had gone to work. It was amazing how empty it was without her. It had never felt empty before she moved in. I suppose that was because when I lived there on my own it was still Frances's flat as far as I was concerned. Now no remnants of Frances remained. Funny, I still visited her grave when I had to think things through, so she was still in my mind, but not in the flat. No, it was more than that. I used to ask her what she would do. She had all this MI6 and MI5 experience and a unique way of looking at things that was different from mine, so it was useful talking to her even if she was dead. I can't remember exactly when I found I could talk to Frances – well, I asked the questions when at the graveyard and the ideas just came. I suppose it was after I killed Mr Wharton and Tug Wilson when they tried to rape me in prison, but it was only in the graveyard near her grave that understanding was clear. One day, they – the ubiquitous 'they' – will lock me up.

Pauline Byford, the psychiatrist, sorted me out but I knew I was way off base when I came out of prison. I didn't think about telling her that I could relate to the way Frances thought, though. There was a seat near her grave and the graveyard was quiet though streets full of cars surrounded it. I sat there in the odd quiet. It was more lonely than quiet with the dull rumbling sounds of cars merging into a grumbling, consistently low-key, disembodied background, which allowed me to get my thinking in order. Perhaps her thoughts to my thoughts were part of that discordant background.

I quickly packed an overnight bag, just in case, and left Sam a note, a short love note. I'd never done that before. I couldn't ring her; private calls to the chambers were strictly verboten between nine and five.

Twenty minutes later I was on the A4 Great West Road, heading west out of London, heading for the M4. It was easy to clear a route with just my blues going and my three point five, series three BMW sport cruising in the fast lane at a steady hundred. Mind you, occasionally you have a dreamer cruising at the correct seventy, or slower, in that lane with apparently no idea what a rear view mirror is for and I had to hit both my blues and two to clear the route. M4 onto the M5 and soon I was in the primitive – or is it the aboriginal – lands of the West Country where the traffic seems to speed up and the thinking slows down.

I arrived at Heartlybridge Police Station about ten minutes to two, so hungry that I was thinking of eating my fingers but the desk sergeant, who had not been made aware they had a murder in the area, got me a sandwich.

94

Kitty and Gaygan were not there yet. Kitty hadn't involved Gaygan much in this case as he was handling some other things for her. I gave her a call on my mobile and as I did she drove in, or rather Gaygan drove her in. She asked the desk sergeant for Chief Inspector Snowden. The sergeant had no idea who she was or why she was here so a muddle ensued. That sorted, and with some clear directions, we quickly found CI Snowden, the man in charge.

He was young, early thirties with a West Country accent. His uniform was immaculate, almost as if it was brand new, straight from the tailor. His black hair was perhaps a little long with a parting down the centre (I'd always found men with a centre parting a little weird), and when he spoke his head was tipped back so that his dark brown eyes seemed to look down his nose and you could look up his large oval nostrils. We shook hands and he demonstrated that he'd read a description of the power shake or some such rubbish without recognising that he was shaking hands with another person.

Kitty smiled at the chief inspector. 'Would you brief us on the crime scene and the victim?'

'I'll have the girl from Exeter brief you.'

'Girl from Exeter?' said Kitty.

'I asked for an experienced detective and they send me a girl who has nothing but a useless degree.' I felt warning signals. Clearly 'girls' were second-class citizens, and having a degree was clearly an obstruction to job skills.

'Well, if she is not competent perhaps you could brief us?' suggested Kitty. I just knew he would duck out. We had belted down here because the superintendent in Exeter was on the ball and now it was like wading through treacle.

'No, she'd best do it. Good experience for her.' I had the impression that he was a prat and a man who never got his hands dirty. I wondered if he had seen the body.

'Do you have other CID officers?'

His expression was one that indicated Kitty shouldn't ask such questions. 'Why do you ask?'

'If she is inexperienced and probably needs supervision perhaps a more experienced officer might have been appropriate?' I thought Kitty was on dangerous ground. She sounded critical.

'Well, I have DS Brownlow but he was away with a DC dealing with some sheep stealing.' I was struggling with this. A murder, and the senior man is dealing with sheep stealing? He had avoided looking at me during this conversation; in fact he had ignored me after the first introductions.

'Perhaps this DC would brief us, then? What is her name?'

'Parks, DC Parks.'

'Her first name?' Kitty was now pushing it. She didn't like Snowden.

'I have no idea, I just expect junior officers to do their job.' No, I didn't like this prat either. Ah well, we all have our prejudices and peccadilloes. For me his peccadillo was stupidity, but perhaps that was my prejudice with regards to him. He was the lord of this manor; that was how he wanted to be seen, senior and superior to all around him, and we were unwanted and inconsequential intruders.

Snowden directed us to a conference room but didn't accompany us. We had to pass the desk sergeant so we asked him DC Parks' name. It was Alison.

Kitty, Gaygan and I sat in an interview room and Alison Parks came in. She was very nervous. We introduced ourselves, shook her hand and called her Alison.

I don't know what she'd been told but whatever it was clearly indicated that we were some form of dangerous aliens. Her fine-cropped black hair framed her oval face, with high cheekbones, giving the impression that she was easy to impress, but her intelligent eyes belied that. Her long black-mascaraed lashes blinked over emerald green eyes, framed by slightly curved eyebrows. Her small, well-shaped, red-shaded lips closed over perfectly straight, white teeth. She should never have been given this job. It needed, at minimum, an experienced detective sergeant.

She fidgeted, twiddling her fingers, and said, 'The scene of the murder is in the village of, um well, Ipplden. I'll spell that: I-P-P-L-den. It had been a village for, yes, estate workers and miners in a local mine way back in the seventeen hundreds. I think it was tin, mined that is.' She stood on one leg then put her foot down. She was very nervous. I wasn't surprised really. 'The village is, well, quite small. Mainly old cottages, you know, and a few new holiday homes and a few, sort of, immediately post-war bungalows.' She took short intakes of breath at inappropriate times, probably due to the tension she was under. I stayed quiet. Eventually she would get there as she settled but it was frustrating. 'In the village is a cobbled mews of stables and, like, garages. They were to keep carts and things in. They're now garages for, well, cars.' She smiled a shy smile at her own obvious statement. 'Above them are flats built of, you know, wood. I was surprised it was still standing. I mean it looked like it shouldn't have, well, survived a strong wind, so appearance is, sort of, deceptive.'

All we needed was a quick overview. There must have been a reason that she was giving this detail and her meaningless fillers didn't help. I once had a boss who in this sort of situation would pull out a newspaper and start to read it. Not helpful.

'Apparently, somebody had actually found a body in one of the flats and told the local plods, who called in the CID.'

See, Jake, prejudice is rife even in someone well educated and young.

'I was sent up here, you know, as they hadn't had much experience of, well, you know, murder.'

'Have you had experience of a murder investigation?' asked Kitty.

'Well, um, no, ma'am.'

'So why did they send you?'

'Wait!' I said.

Kitty and Alison looked at me. I suppose my abrupt interruption startled them.

'Alison, I want you to walk over to the window and look out. Think for a minute or two about what you can see out there. Don't think about us just think about what you can see and then take three deep breaths; in through your nose and slowly out through your mouth. If I were to ask you what out there might be important to me think about your answer. Then think about this murder and what you need to tell us.' I paused and she was uptight. 'And then just relax and do it.'

She did as I said and I watched her walk to the window with a straight back, head held high, short strides and no wobble on her over-high, high-heeled shoes. She had pride; it showed. I was impressed. She looked out of the window and I saw her take the deep breaths and she blew out inflating her cheeks. She looked round. I nodded and smiled.

'Okay?'

She nodded and returned to her position but did not sit; she was relaxed.

'Don't worry, Alison,' I said. 'Kitty here is an expert in murder investigations and I've killed a few people, so all in all, it should be all right.'

She smiled. She thought I was kidding about me being a killer. 'Oh that's good then,' she said. You could see the tension decrease even more in her body.

'Alison perhaps it would be better to take us to the crime scene and brief us there.'

98

19

We walked to the village from the police station. It was an old village. I had the feeling that everyone would know strangers from London were here by six this evening.

'Why were you sent on this job, Alison?'

'I don't suppose I should say this but Chief Inspector Snowden is a local and they don't think much of him in Exeter. Every time something happens he screams for help and the super there is pissed off, so he sent me so the chief inspector couldn't blame the CID in Exeter if it was a cock up. They also wanted to show they co-operated but the super got you lot involved.'

We stopped at the end of an old cobbled mews.

'What's your view of Chief Inspector Snowden?'

Clearly, Kitty thought I shouldn't ask that question as she frowned at me, but I had to get Alison integrated with us.

Alison didn't know what to say. She then threw caution to the wind and said, 'He's a wanker.' It was said in a disparaging tone that increased the condemnation.

Kitty laughed. 'Is that from personal observation, Alison?'

'Oh no, I meant–' She stopped, coloured and said, 'Sorry.'

'Okay, which cottage?' asked Kitty, laughing. .

'Number five.' She pointed. There was no crime scene tape across the door.

'No tape, Alison.'

'No, well they didn't have any and the chief inspector said it would be all right.'

'There's a DS here. Why didn't he do the investigation?' I asked. She looked at the floor. 'Alison?'

'Well, DS John Brownlow is a nice guy, very experienced, helpful and that, but he doesn't get on with the chief inspector so he's sent on all the local crap jobs. He's always been in the city, Exeter and Plymouth, till he came here and he gets put on all the country jobs and he knows nothing about the country and he retires this year.'

'And the DC?'

'Yes, well, he is from the country and he's good as well.'

'But?'

'I don't know really.'

There was no movement in the mews. No uniformed police officers guarding the place.

'Scene of crime officers, Alison?' asked Kitty.

'Well, they're not here yet.'

'Where are they?'

'Well, I told the chief inspector I needed them and he said he would arrange it, then he said he would wait for you to arrive.'

'Alison. Get the forensic team here now and I want four uniformed officers to seal this place off.'

'Yes, ma'am.'

This was the first scene of crime I had ever been to where there were no uniformed police officers.

'Alison. Make notes. I want a step-by-step timed record of everything that happens, who arrives when, what they are doing, who is keeping their record about what.'

'Yes, ma'am.' Alison was on her radio, clear and authoritative.

Four officers arrived and Kitty briefed them and they secured the area. We waited and a uniformed inspector arrived. He stood like a spare part and Kitty ignored him.

'Has anybody been in there Alison?'

'Yes ma'am. I have.'

'Stay just there. Gaygan, find the person who found the body and get their story.'

'Yes, boss.' He went off to where Alison directed him with a uniformed officer. This was a dog's breakfast. Still it was a hick village where the most exciting thing that has happened is a kid fell off his bike or the local drunk fell in the duck pond, again.

'Go on with the story please, Alison,' I said. This really was a dysfunctional team due to poor leadership.

Alison was now in control of herself. She had at last recognised that we were not ogres.

'The chief inspector said something like, "This'll be some real experience for you, girly. Get in there and observe the scene." I hate it when he calls me "girly".' She paused, thought and started again. 'I suppose it was about nine last night. It had been an overcast day so it was darkish. The streetlights were not yet on, not that you could see much if they were on as they're converted gaslights. We walked to the front door; it was open. It didn't look as if it had been forced. I knocked and called out anyway. The local police just laughed at me. There were four of them but none came with me. I was bloody scared and I suppose it showed.

'I went through the door. Inside there's a very short passage and it was pitch black. On the left is a door into the stable or garage area. That door was shut but not locked,' said Alison. 'I didn't go in. I thought one of the locals should come with me and check in there but none did.' Her presentation was now smooth, delivered at a steady, confident pace with no fillers. This was a bright young woman.

'Who was in charge?' asked Kitty.

'Well, the chief inspector was supposed to be but he wasn't there and a uniformed inspector, Inspector Marshall, was in charge, I suppose.'

The 'I suppose' was a clincher. This inexperienced officer had been left on her own when any decent policeman would have nursed her through, ensured the routine and, above all, protected her against the chance that the killer was still in the building, or at least reassured her that he or she was not.

'Wait one minute, Alison. Did you ask for help?'

'No, sir.'

'Okay. In future, remember in an investigation such as this one, request of the senior person the support you need. Every officer has equal responsibility as part of an investigation team even if they have different jobs. Standing around isn't one of their jobs. You have additional training and need to use it. One or more of the other officers should have been with you. But once the scene has been secured then the forensic team goes in. Ask for support to get the people needed here, that should have been done last night.'

'Yes, sir. I knew that, sir, but the chief inspector...' Her voice petered out.

'Are you Inspector Marshall?' Kitty asked the uniformed officer.

'Yes, ma'am.' Attitude indicated resentment.

'Inspector, the house-to-house last night; have you completed the report?'

'The Chief Inspector said–'

'The answer to that question is either yes or no, so what is it?'

'It is not completed.'

'Has it shown anything of note yet?'

'No and I resent...'

'Good, get used to it. I am the SIO here and I want that report complete before the SOCO and the forensic team arrive. They may need what your officers find. I'd like to see the report of the search of the garage, the mews and the area behind the mews in the vicinity of the crime, and what the house-to-house revealed, what strange cars have been driven into the village during the past week and descriptions of the people in them.'

'Yes, ma'am.' For the first time he appreciated Kitty was in charge. It then dawned on me that Kitty and Alison were the only female officers I had seen and Gaygan was the only non-white officer. I wondered!

'Go on please, Alison. What happened next?' Kitty's voice was again quiet and supportive. She was focussed on Alison Parks and the girl straightened her back and closed her hands. She was now filled with the confidence that here were people who really were interested in what she saw. She was important, or at least what she saw was. The inspector was on his radio.

'There was a narrow stairway in front of us. The treads were bare wood and worn.'

'Us? Alison.'

'Me, ma'am.'

'On your own?'

'Yes, ma'am.' A uniformed sergeant listening to this was clearly embarrassed. So there were some professionals here.

Alison was continuing. 'I tried the light switch but the light didn't work.'

'Were you wearing gloves?' asked Kitty.

'Yes, ma'am, and I only touched the end of the switch as I'd been trained to.'

'Good. Go on.'

'Nervously I started up the stairs. Then this furry thing slipped down the stairs; it's green eyes shone in the torchlight. I was frightened fartless.'

A chuckle came from Kitty and me. We'd both been there so we knew exactly how she felt and her phraseology captured it.

'It was a bloody cat. The stairs are very narrow, only wide enough for one person and we – I – had to duck at the first-floor level to climb them.'

20

Police transport pulled into the mews as Alison finished speaking. It was SOCO and the forensic bods. The forensic team dressed in paper suits and coveralls entered the mews cottage. Similarly dressed, we followed them. The stairs were as described by Alison. The room we entered was the full width of the building with a window at each end looking out on to the front and back. It was about 4 or 4.5 metres wide with a door in the middle of the wall opposite the top of the stairs. It was a kitchen/diner and sitting room. It had a very old gas stove next to a sink at the front end; some cupboards, a table covered with an oilcloth with kitchen chairs around it in the middle, and a sort of settee thing with a TV at the back end. The floor was covered with lino and the walls seemed to be distempered blue. The light had been switched on and it worked. There was one bare bulb in the middle of the room. There was no indication of a disturbance in that room.

'Was it like this when you came in?' I asked Alison.
'Yes, sir.'
'No sign of any struggle or disturbance?'
'No, sir.'
'Your conclusion?'
'The victim probably walked in.'
'Reason you say that?'
'Well, she would be difficult to carry up the stairs.'
'Okay.'

'What were your thoughts?'

'I can remember exactly. I was scared. Something my granddad said came to mind – "Sod this for a game of soldiers".' We laughed. 'I was terrified. There was something behind that door and I had no idea what I'd see when I opened it. It was ajar; open only a few inches. Whoever had found the body had not shut the door. I pushed it, gently. It swung open slowly and creaked just like in a horror film. I thought I was going to wet myself. Then I thought about those bastards in the mews, got angry and was back in control of myself.'

The door was fully open now.

'Good. Go on then,' I said.

I had to smile. She was reliving what had happened and the way she felt. I suppose I have a store of those sorts of memories, when the emotions are running high, but I couldn't remember a situation where a uniformed officer wasn't at the scene before me. This really was a badly disciplined unit.

Alison said, 'I pushed the door and it swang open. The room was dark. There is a window to the left but the curtains were pulled. There was a wall to the right of the door with a door in it. I switched on the light.' The room was as Alison described.

'Tell us what you saw.'

'My torch shone on a body. The victim was corporal Celia Foley. She was as you can see now, naked, sitting astride a kitchen chair, sitting on it backwards.'

The forensic team were taking photos and a pathologist was inspecting the body. Alison continued, 'She was facing away from the door so I could only see her back. Her legs were tied to the back legs of the chair, her hands were tied together and her arms were tied above the elbows to the backrest at the back of the chair. Her head lolled forward. The chair had no seat so her backside protruded through.

105

There were a couple of candles in holders on the floor below the chair. From the burn marks she'd been tortured. Her pubic hair had been burned away and she was heavily blistered and had raw open wounds.' Alison was reliving what she saw and was very distraught but did not cry. The forensic people were taking more photos and that reduced the horrific impact of what we could see.

'By burning her sexual organs and backside?' said Kitty.

'Yes, ma'am. She also had cigarette burns on her back.' These we could see. 'I found the light switch, switched it on and walked around the victim's body. Her nipples and her bust had been burned; cigarette burns. Blood from her face had run into her chest. The smell was awful.' It still was, apart from the fact that the windows were now open. 'There were flies all over her and buzzing. I didn't know what had actually killed her. I was so shocked and sick that I didn't care. I ran back into the kitchen and was sick in the sink. I splashed water on my face.'

There were now powerful lights in the room and the forensic people were doing minute scans. One was carefully putting the candles and candlesticks into plastic lined boxes, securing them and sealing the boxes and making notes.

'What happened next, Alison?'

'Snowden was there. He must have arrived and come up. All he said was, "Well?" So I reported. I think I can remember exactly what I said.'

'Go on then, Alison. You're doing well,' I said.

She nodded, thought and then said, 'Woman: early thirties, dead, tied to a chair, has been tortured using flame from a candle and cigarettes to burn her. Probably been dead a few days, I said, and then he said, "Well done, Constable. We'll see what the forensic people have to say and then we'll go and collar the killer. Go write your report".'

'Did the chief inspector go into the room?' I asked.

'No, sir.'

There was nothing we could observe that would add to what Alison had said. The pathologists inspecting the body would do a post-mortem later today.

'Is there anything you noticed as odd, out of place, unexpected?' I asked.

Alison was thinking; there was something. Kitty went to speak. I held up my hand to stop her.

'Yes, sir.'

'What?'

'Well. It was her nails. You know, girls are particular about their nails.'

'And?'

'The nails on her left hand had been cut back; only her index finger, middle finger and ring finger. The rest were, well, as they should be, rounded, protruding past the end of the finger but those three had been cut back, sort of square to the quick and the corners cut off, not filed or anything.'

'Any view about that?'

'She scratched him.'

'Left hand?'

'Perhaps she was left-handed.'

'Well, we will look for scratches on the right side of the face and neck of any suspect. Well observed, Alison.'

Kitty spoke to the pathologist. He was circumspect.

'It looks as if she has been tortured. By burning with the candles. This would have caused considerable pain. If this had been done to extract information there is no doubt she would have given it. Before the torture with the flames she appears to have been raped but we cannot confirm that at this stage. She was also beaten with what was probably a bamboo cane and punched in the face. The victim has been dead at least three days. But we will confirm what I have said.'

107

'Cause of death, doctor?'

'Most likely manual strangulation from the front. The marks are consistent with that method but we will confirm the cause of death during the post-mortem.'

'When will we know?'

'You can observe the post-mortem and the report will be with you first thing in the morning.'

I felt like shit but Kitty wanted to view the post-mortem. I suggested Alison should go with her and I went and booked rooms in a local hotel where Alison was staying.

The next morning Alison came into the room we had adopted as our office.

'Have the pathology people said how she died?' Kitty asked.

'Yes, Inspector. Dr Markham, he's the forensic pathologist, said she was strangled and died of asphyxia due to strangulation. She had a fractured hyoid bone in the neck and soft tissue haemorrhage extending downward to the level of the right thyroid cartilage. Well, that's what Dr Markham said. He said that the killer had probably done this before. She'd been raped both vaginally and anally but there was no evidence of semen. Her body had been shaved before any sexual activity. The body was also thoroughly cleaned with alcohol, probably methylated spirits, so there was no DNA or fingerprints on her. There was evidence of severe beating with some form of cane across the buttocks, most probably bamboo. She'd been repeatedly punched in the face with a gloved fist: a brown leather glove.'

'Any damage to the ears?'

Alison looked at me in surprise. 'Yes. She was wearing earrings and the pins that go through the ears had torn on the left lob.'

'The torture, was it before or after the rape?'

'Ah, yes. Dr Markham said he thought she'd been raped and beaten, then tortured then strangled.'

'You said earlier the pubic hair had been burned away.'

'Yes, I was wrong. Her pubic hair had been shaved; not what I'd assumed was, well, torture burns.'

'Alison, you said that blood had run down her face onto her chest. You also said she had been cleaned with alcohol. What does that tell you?'

She thought. 'The punching was after the cleaning.'

'Was there much blood?'

'No, sir.'

'So?'

'The punching was after death.'

'How did you know her name?' I asked.

'A tattoo on her shoulder showed she was RMP. We did a check, missing persons on the national database, and her name came up.'

'Did you see the tattoo when you went into the room or did you go back in?'

'I went back in, sir, and made notes.'

'Let me get this right, you went into the room, saw a woman tied to a chair who had been tortured, you came out, reported to Chief Inspector Snowden then went back into the room and made notes?'

'Yes, sir.'

'Good, that took some guts, but you went back in alone?'

'Yes, sir.'

'Where was Chief Inspector Snowden?'

'Outside, sir.'

'Alison, about the tattoo: when you said we did a check, who was the we?'

'DS Brownlow suggested it and I did it.'

'Well done, Alison. You did a great job.' I was boiling. I looked at Kitty. She shook her head; she knew what I was thinking.

Kitty said, 'So, Jake, we've another one and it couldn't be

Carmichael or Phillips so it has to be Wright or Holt.' This confirmed my thinking.

Surprisingly, it was Alison who spoke next. 'There are some problems with this if the torture occurred in that room,' she said.

'Go on,' said Kitty.

'The screams. You apply a flame to somebody and they'll scream.'

'I'd like you to follow up on that, Alison. Get the neighbours checked out to find out what they heard. The uniformed officers will have done that but do it again, and have an experienced uniformed officer with you,' said Kitty.

'Thank you, Alison. You've done a great job giving us all the information we needed.'

She smiled in relief and relaxed.

21

Later that afternoon, after we had read the various reports, all the relevant people were assembled in a briefing room. Kitty was at the front and in the room was CI Snowden, Sergeant Gaygan Gupta, DC Alison Parks, Inspector Marshall, five other uniformed officers, the sergeant who was at the scene, DS Brownlow, DC Everett and me.

Kitty started off, thanking them for involving us. She outlined the main facts of this case and the match to a series of other cases. She then went into the specifics of the previous cases, explaining our investigations into the serial murders and commonalities, and the reduction from six hundred and two suspects to just four. She then spoke about the murders of people who had suggested a particular perpetrator. The local police were having difficulty in comprehending what they were hearing. I knew how they felt and I was in the middle of it.

'Now I'm going to tell you something about your local killing. The murdered woman was Celia Foley. Celia was a corporal in the RMP so did not have the class profile of the others, but there are other striking similarities between her killing and the other killings: she suffered what the other victims suffered except she was also tortured, using a candle flame to her genitalia and cigarette burns to her breasts and back.' Kitty paused for a long time and looked at everybody in the room. She wanted what had happened here to sink in. A few faces were distinctly green.

111

'We think we know why she was tortured. We think the killer wanted to know what Sergeant Billinghurst, the murdered RMP sergeant, knew, but Celia knew nothing. As I said, her killing has eliminated the dead suspects and brought us down to four. One is a female, so it is very unlikely – possible, but very unlikely. So that brings us to three. The location of one of them at the time of this killing is known so that brings us down to two.

'The problem we have is this; even if we know which of the two is the killer the evidence we have is circumstantial. It's compelling but circumstantial. We need something concrete. We're going to chase leads that we have but you can deliver this murderer because it's relatively fresh and it occurred on your patch. Anything and everything you find may be the evidence that nails this bastard.'

She scanned the people in the room to ensure that what she'd just said had registered. 'It's possible that Celia was not killed in the room where she was found. We've not reviewed the forensics of the room or your report of the surrounding area covering house-to-house et cetera. Our conclusion is based on the fact that somebody who is burned will scream. There's no evidence that her mouth was bound with tape but some other gag could have been used. However, it would have to have been removed for her to answer questions, so her silence could not have been completely controlled.' Kitty surveyed the group again.

'We're asking you to go back over everything you've done, the area, the door-to-doors, strangers in the area over the period we think this occurred. You've got photos of the murdered woman and photos of five men. Two are dead, one has been cleared and one of the other two is our killer or maybe two are. I'll say one other thing, and listen very carefully: you've heard what we've done so far and you'll note that not one solitary item of this has appeared in the press apart from the killing down here. We know that was a legitimate press release. If one item of what I've told you is leaked to the press we'll put our specialist hound on to finding who leaked it. And he's good, bloody good. The press are interested and they'll pay crispy notes for information. If it leaks he'll find out who leaked it and we'll take action to ensure that officer will be in deep, deep shit, and their career ended. Do I make myself clear? That officer is already among the press people here. That may surprise you. The press boys are bloody good and they give us leads and it's our boyo that picks up those leads. Do not discuss this with your wives, girlfriends, mates or other officers outside of this room.' Kitty looked around the room. At least two officers looked away. 'Remember, your job but, more importantly, the lives of others could be on the line. Chief Inspector Snowden has agreed that DC Parks will be our liaison. Just keep her in the loop and remember we've had two police officers murdered on this case so far, so I suggest you guard your arses and make certain Alison sees all the information. She'll send me summaries and talk to me every day. Any questions?'

There were a few questions but these people were out of their depth and in shock. They had a horrendous murder on their hands and now found out it was part of something much bigger. After doing her best to answer their concerns, Kitty closed the meeting and we left soon after.

'I thought that went well, Kitty. What do you think, Alison?'

'Do you really have a man in among the press?'

'Why? Are you thinking of selling them information?' Kitty asked.

'Oh, no! I'd just not heard of that before.'

'And nor has anybody else.' Kitty smiled and so did Alison.

'What do you think, Jake?' asked Kitty.

'That lot couldn't find grass on a village green.'

113

'Ah, you're so picturesque, strikingly negative and probably correct.'

I followed Kitty and Gaygan to a service station on the motorway and we had our own debrief. In the discussion, only one thing emerged for me to do and that was to talk to Gzifa Sherzai, the woman in Afghanistan asking about her missing sister, Muna. That was not going to be easy as we only had an email address. By the time we'd sorted out what we were going to do it was late and I headed for home, driving much faster than I should. But I didn't get in until gone 11 p.m.

I sat on a stool in the kitchen while Sam worked magic with tomatoes and minced beef and then put pasta on to boil. If anybody had told me that Sam was domesticated, let alone a fantastic homemaker, I'd have just laughed. She had everything: beauty, patience, social skills, education, but I would never have imagined her up to her elbows in washing-up water, ploughing through a pile of ironing or sewing a zip into a pair of jeans. She was magic and I must have done something extraordinarily well in a past life to end up with her.

She'd been asleep when I got in, not in bed but on the settee in front of the television in her nightclothes. She insisted on getting me some food. I'm a simple kind of guy and would have been happy with a cup of tea and a jam sandwich, mainly because that was about the extent of my culinary skills, apart from cornflakes. I was really good with cornflakes, using just the right amount of milk or one of those little runny yogurt things and sugar. No, with Sam, it had to be a proper meal. My mother had been like that. If you're going to eat you'll eat properly and clean your plate. No, Sam did not insist I cleaned my plate but I always did. It was a value built in from childhood – waste not, want not.

I watched her as she cooked and couldn't help noticing that her nightdress hung on her like a misshapen shroud and her face was creased with sleep. How on earth could a woman as accomplished and beautiful as Sam be prepared to put up with a randomly inconsiderate, work-obsessed bum like me? Yes, randomly inconsiderate. I wasn't inconsiderate all the time. I just loved her. She just did everything a perfect wife would do and we weren't even married, and she'd never pressurised me into getting married. It had crossed my mind that perhaps she didn't want to get married and she'd never mentioned children. In fact, I didn't even know how she felt about children.

She scooped the penne into a bowl and poured in the sauce. She then ground on the pepper and grated Parmigiano over the top. If she was going to do something, she was going to do it properly.

The best thing about watching her prepare this meal was her bum. By some inexplicable mischance, the hem at the back of her nightdress was caught at her waist so her bum was exposed. I wasn't going to tell her; I just enjoyed being a voyeur. Sam had this fantastic bum. It was firm and round, sort of jutted out at the top, then it went round smoothly and then her legs flowed downwards. I had never been a connoisseur of bums but if I had I'm sure I would have rated this as the best bum in the whole world.

She brought the hot plate to the table in front of me and then sat down. I had to laugh at the shock on her face as her bum hit the cold of the wooden seat.

'You bastard!' she laughed. 'You've been looking at my bum.'

'This penne is fantastic and so is your bum,' I smiled and she threw the dishtowel at me. Oh, a perfect end to a less than perfect day.

22

The next morning found the three of us, Kitty, Gaygan and me, in Soho outside Eromeni, the gay bar where Gabriel Holt, one of our two prime suspects, worked; well, he was part owner. The ladies of the night were gone, business completed, the drunks had staggered away and a few street dwellers were rolled up in plastic bags or cardboard igloos in selected doorways. The early morning air in the shadow of the damp buildings was grey with the unique chill of a London morning. Yes, it was cold and dreary.

Kitty and Gaygan went in. Five minutes later they came out and Holt got in the back of the car with me.

'Aw, Captain, this is cosy.'

'You two behave yourselves,' quipped Kitty. 'I'll have no shenanigans in the back of a police car,' she joked but it was forced. There was something wrong.

'See, you're getting me into trouble with miss already, Captain, and me only an innocent ex-private.'

I smiled, but decided to side-step the banter. 'What does Eromeni mean, Gabriel?' I asked.

'Oow, you are lovely, Captain. You even know my name.' He smiled at me, rocked his head from side to side and made his mouth into the shape of a kiss, closing his lips and pulling his head back with a little shake. 'Perhaps we could meet for a teeny weeny drinky soon.'

'You two fucking behave yourselves and shut the fuck up.' There was an edge in Kitty's voice. It was louder than usual

116

and she spoke more quickly, but she softened it when repeating my question. 'What *does* Eromeni mean?' It seemed she was trying to control her anger.

'I thought it's obvious.' He tossed his head back in an expression of contempt used by extrovert homosexuals. 'Lover Boys, of course.' I supposed it was obvious when you looked at the word.

'Good, now we know, just keep silent until we get to the factory.' The anger was again evident. We were both silent and Gaygan drove in silence. 'The better part of valour is discretion,' to quote or misquote Shakespeare, but the ambience was becoming oppressive. I wondered why she was irritable. She was now silent in the car and had not really spoken apart from the rebuke and normal greetings, which had been perfunctory. This was not the Kitty that I'd started to know. Something had happened last night or this morning.

We got out of the car at the police station and she told Gaygan to take Gabriel Holt to interview room 2. Gabriel walked, pin-toed with a light step and exaggerated hip movements. He didn't do that in the army or the drill sergeant would have had a fit. So was this the real Gabriel or was he acting?

'What's up, Kitty?'

'You! That's what's fucking up.'

'What have I done?'

'You told your secret service chums some cock and bull story and now I've Superintendent fucking West on my back.'

'Hang on, Detective Inspector. One: I've no idea what you're talking about, and two: I don't expect to be addressed in the way you're talking to me.'

She stopped and looked at me. There was a mixture of anger and doubt in her pushed-out lips and stance.

'You didn't tell West our findings at Heartlybridge and that–'

'Stop right there, Detective Inspector. This is basically your case. I'm in it for the ride, the links to The Family and the links to the army. I've two people I'll give information to: one in the army because we need his co-operation and he's helped us, but he's not interested in any detail as you've seen. The other is Sir Barrow Jones, but I've given no information to either of them. If we've a leak it's not from me but I know West and as you know he's a creature of The Family.'

'What about Rupert Carmichael?'

'I told you about that contact.'

'And you didn't speak to him last night?'

'Not last night or this morning. I left you and went home.'

She was, I think the right word is, appalled.

'Christ, I'm sorry, Jake.'

'Now tell me what's happened.'

'When I got in this morning West was with my new boss.'

'Who is?'

'Superintendent Urmee Khan. They were very pally. West knew everything and my boss told me I had to keep West informed of all actions we take and what we plan to do. If necessary he'll attend, as it could involve a member of the Cabinet. I thought you'd briefed him.'

'Thanks for the vote of confidence, Kitty.' I was now miffed. 'Let me make a call and then I'll join you. I'd be careful about your boss and Chief Inspector Snowden, and tell West nothing, ever. I've briefed you on him in the past.'

She nodded. 'I'm sorry, Jake.'

Two minutes later, I was talking to Barrow. I told him the situation and that I wanted West off Kitty's back. I wanted her boss to know that this was a criminal case that may have had potential political ramifications and MI5 would deal

118

with them. In the event of political problems arising, we had an authorised Special Branch liaison contact, Chief Inspector Wilkes, SCD attached to the Serious and Organised Crime Agency. Barrow listened, tested a couple of things, asked a couple of questions and told me to get on with the job and he would contact me if I needed to know anything. That was, as far as I was concerned, West fixed. The other two we couldn't gag. I found Kitty in the canteen and told her all of this.

'I'm really sorry, Jake. I should have known better by now and thank you. I keep forgetting that you've a lot of pull. Shall we go and interview lover boy?'

23

When we went into the interview room I realised that
Gabriel Holt looked nothing like the pictures we had from
his army records. He was slimmer and wearing lipstick. His
hair had been dyed black and was long and shaped so that it
swept back covering his ears and stopped in a curve just
level with his shoulders. His eyebrows were black and his
eyelashes were made up with mascara. His eyes had blue eye
shadow but it couldn't hide the fact that he was tired, having been working in the bar to the early hours, and he'd
probably not been to bed. His clothes were black. He was
wearing a Crombie, black, unlined leather jacket over a
black cotton shirt with white pearl buttons; smart, fine, wool
trousers with razor-sharp creases and a black belt with a
silver buckle. He had shiny, black, slip-on leather shoes with
a silver chain across the front, and black socks. He was
wearing some discrete jewellery: a silver earring in his left
ear, a fine silver chain around his neck and plain silver rings
on his pinkies. On his right wrist he had a silver bangle and
on his left a black-faced watch with a black leather strap: the
man in black with silver trim. It was strange; the effect of the
army was clear to see and so was the effeminate, extrovert,
friendly and, I must say, likeable personality that we were
faced with.

'I do like your jacket, Gabriel.'

'Oow, yes, it's lovely. It was a present.'

'From a client?'

120

'Oow, no, from his wife.'

What do you say? I'll never understand the inhabitants of the twilight world. The wife of a client of Gabriel gave him a beautiful leather jacket that must have cost well over £1000. Kitty looked at me and raised her eyebrows. I shrugged.

'Can I see your hands, Gabriel?'

He held out his hands palm down. I turned them over. He was looking at them then he raised his head to look at me. There were no scratches on his hands and none that I could see on his face or neck.

Now we were into the interview there were no extravagant gestures or homosexual, effeminate pronunciation; just easy, gentle, intelligent responses, but he was no pushover and I couldn't describe him as compliant.

We questioned Gabriel about Washington and broadened it to the other killings. We played every game in the book with him. We made him feel safe. We leaned on him, lied to him, reassured him and threatened him. He just denied all knowledge of any killing at any time by any person at any place. However, I had this feeling; I knew he knew about the killings and he was bringing into play his whole experience of hiding, as he hid his sexuality in the army, and despite my proficiency I could not get through the barrier. I couldn't even find a crack.

As far as he was concerned, during the day, Michael Carmichael was rarely out of his sight and at night Michael Carmichael was rarely out of his bed. Yes, Michael Carmichael was a bad boy who ran a drug-smuggling business. Michael Carmichael was a hero who risked his life for his country and was a highly successful leader of men. Sergeant Jason Phillips killed Carmichael, but Carmichael had never been alone with a woman let alone killed one. But, but there was something; I could feel the intangibility of it. There was an odourless smell; I could hear it in the silence of the things left unsaid. My nerve endings were tingling but

121

there was nothing stimulating them. Don't tell my granny, rest her soul; she would say that I'd inherited The Gift, whatever that was. Ultimately, I was willing to believe that Carmichael was innocent. Rupert Carmichael's description of his son made Michael Carmichael a very unlikely serial killer and Gabriel's evidence supported that view but there was something – something. Let's change tack; let's reverse things.

'Okay, I'm convinced. It wasn't Michael, so it must have been you.'

I felt Kitty react next to me but she was immediately onside. Gabriel looked surprised. It hadn't even crossed his mind that the consequence of the killer not being Michael would mean it was him.

'Me!' The shock and surprise could be heard in his voice.

'Yes, you. You've convinced me that Michael Carmichael killed none of these women and we know he couldn't have killed Corporal Foley because he was dead and you weren't. So the conclusion I must reach is that it was you.'

Kitty stepped in. 'I think before we continue questioning you, we'll need to caution you and we advise you to get a solicitor. We'll tell you that formally when we caution you but you might like to get a solicitor before we take any further action.'

He just looked numb. 'You think I could kill a woman?' he spat, indignant, but again there was something wrong. Was he really shocked? Yes, he was, but it was not about swapping the Carmichael accusation to him; it was something else, something deeper.

'You could kill a man. You've killed men.'

'Yes, but that's different and I was a soldier.'

Kitty said, 'Gabriel, all the evidence we have pointed at Michael. Your evidence convinces us, as Jake said, that as you claim you were with Michael day and night at the places and times the women were murdered, our conclusion must be that you did it.'

His eyes filled with tears. It was so strange. Why was he so emotional? His mascara started to run leaving black streaks on his cheeks. Was it possible that he did do it? Never! Even I couldn't believe he could kill at least seven women and perhaps many more. Yet, he was cracking.

'It must have been Wrighty.'

At last, a crack.

'Are you saying it was Malcolm Wright?' Kitty was pressing. We were getting somewhere.

'I don't know.'

'Tell us what you do know.' She was now playing him like a fish on a line. Keep the line just taut with no jerks nor too much tension.

'I can't.'

'I understand you want to, but something's stopping you.'

'I can't.'

'Come on, Gabriel. I'm sure you can.'

I had a vision of two kids in a playground – 'You can!' 'I can't!' Time to change tack again while he was off balance.

'Okay, Gabriel, now I understand. Michael didn't kill those women. You didn't kill those women. Wright *did* kill those women but he did it for Michael.'

There was a look of horror on his face and surprise on Kitty's face. The tears were now flooding down Gabriel's face. Sobs came from deep inside him.

'Let me tell you what we're going to do. We're going to charge you with accessory before the fact and with accessory after the fact.'

He was lost. He had no idea what I had just said.

'We don't think you're an accomplice but if we think you're continuing to hide something we'll charge you with that as well.'

Fear and confusion induced by words is a great weapon.

He was totally bemused. He had absolutely no idea what I was talking about. What I deduced was that he thought he was in deep trouble and whatever way he went that trouble would follow him. There was guilt there, deep soul-destroying guilt, but about what?

Gaygan gave him a box of tissues. He wiped his streaked face. He was a mess.

'I suggest you ring somebody for a solicitor to defend you.'

'No, Captain, I've got a solicitor. It's, it's Mr Carstairs. He'll be my solicitor.'

'If you're sure, Gabriel. Mr Carstairs isn't a heavyweight and you might need one.' I was driving in the fear. I'd never heard of Carstairs.

'Kitty, this is your province not mine. I reckon you and your sergeant should do this and I'll come and see you when you have it all nailed down.' I was ignoring Gabriel and he was listening. I could see Kitty knew exactly what I was doing.

'But if our boyo gives us the information he just becomes a witness.'

'Does that mean I won't go to prison?' sobbed Gabriel.

'That, I don't know, but you'll have to tell us everything; no secrets, no protecting Michael, just the truth. You'll have to give evidence in court. Are you prepared to do that?'

'Yes, sir.'

'Let me just check. You understand you'll have to appear in court and give evidence?'

'Yes, sir.'

'Just one question, out of interest more than anything else, have you ever met or heard of a woman named Muna?'

'Muna?'

'Yes, Muna.'

'I think so. Yes, she was a friend of a girl that Jase was banging.'

'What was *her* name?'

'I don't really know; it was something like Uzuri.'

'Did Malc go out with Muna?'

'I don't know really.'

'Is that the truth, Gabriel?'

'Yes, sir. Honest, sir.' All resistance had gone. Gabriel was being truthful. He didn't know.

'Thank you. Over to you then, Detective Inspector. Give me a ring in the very unlikely event that you need me.'

I left. There was still something wrong and for the life of me I didn't know what it was. Gabriel Holt was involved. The mystery was how. Gabriel knew who killed the women – or did he just think he did? And I still didn't believe it was Michael Carmichael and my conviction of that was strengthened by Gabriel's evidence, but he was in love with Carmichael so there may have been a distortion there. Wright seemed to be in the frame but the evidence was weak.

24

I sat in the bath. I rarely had baths. My Gran used to joke that only dirty people had baths. I once read that Queen Elizabeth I had two baths a year whether she needed them or not. I supposed I was the same, but I had a shower every morning and after any exercise whether I needed it or not. To me, a bath was a place of contemplation. Navel gazing was the phrase that sprung to mind. I could imagine a famous philosopher laying in his bath gazing at his navel and thinking great thoughts. Not that I was a philosopher, but I did like just relaxing in a bath when I had a problem that just kept whizzing round in my head and going nowhere. Of course I couldn't navel gaze as I'd used Sam's bubble bath stuff and the bath was full of bubbles. I couldn't even sail my rubber duck. Not that I had a rubber duck, but if I did have one it would have been in a fog of bubbles. So I just let the hot water relax me and the bubbles cleanse me and I let my mind gently float through the fog of information.

Assumption: only four people could have committed the murders of the women. No, that was wrong. Five people: Michael Carmichael, Jason Phillips, Gabriel Holt, Malcolm Wright and Susan Thomas. Was that a valid assumption? Could there have been anybody else? Well, of course there could but we'd absolutely nothing to suggest anybody else. Wrong: it could have been Corporal Gill Hibberd but we'd cleared him. I decided I was going to buy a rubber duck, a

126

yellow one. Oh, a life on the ocean waves. Pay attention, Jake.

Assumption: Susan Thomas is a woman. No, that isn't an assumption. Susan Thomas is a woman. It's a fact. Well, I assumed it was a fact and if true it's extremely unlikely that she was the killer. Why? Why should we eliminate her? Female serial killers are extremely rare. I shouldn't have had that second brandy. No, that's wrong. One in six serial killers is a woman but they don't strangle strangers and rape them. I supposed it's possible but unlikely. Oh shit, I'll just cross her off the list.

Assumption: Carmichael and Phillips are dead so they couldn't have... No. Rethink. They could've done all the murders but the last one. No, I'm now convinced it's not Jase or Carmichael. The last one had differences. It had no drugs and it involved torture by flames. Why would somebody torture somebody? Because they were sadistic or wanted to gather specific information or just wanted to find out what somebody knew. So, who would want to know what a police officer knew? Somebody who was concerned about what the police officer knew. What did that tell me? That the killing of Celia Foley could have been a killing disguised as the original killings. So where would that leave us? Confused. How would anybody know the details of the murders so he or she could repeat them? Conclusion: only someone who'd commited the murders or knew the details could mimic the murders. Other than the original killer, it had to be an investigator or somebody who had been told or shown by the killer. Is this helping? Yes, this was driving me further towards Holt and/or Wright.

We still had the situation that Carmichael or Phillips could have been the serial killer. And we had a second killer – Holt or Wright. A shuddering idea came to mind. It could have been Kitty or Gaygan. No, that was ridiculous. Was I making this too complicated? Oh I wished I had a yellow rubber duck. No, I'd decided not Carmichael or Phillips already.

Why would somebody go to the length of torturing somebody to death? To find out what they knew about a serial killing? Probably. Why would they disguise that murder as if it was the same as the serial killings? Two answers: because they are the serial killer, or because they wanted the murder to look like the work of the serial killer.

The door opened and Sam stuck her head in.

I was now absolutely clear. No, yes, whoever did this wanted to know whether they were in the frame for the other murders. This was driven by fear and uncertainty. Yes, it had to be...

'Are you okay in there?'

'I know you just want to come and join me.'

She laughed and came in. She was starkers and got in behind me in the shallow end with her legs on either side of me. She put her arms around me and started to wash the bits she wanted to wash – well, to play with.

'I do love you,' she whispered in my ear and then, in a flash, I knew the answer to one of my questions. As I had the answer I could now do something else. Sod the yellow rubber duck! I had Sam. Oh, a life on the ocean waves. Let's play submarines.

25

I went to see Barrow.

'And what can I do for you this fine morning, Jake?'

'I'd like somebody to talk to a woman in Afghanistan about the murders.'

'I see. Tell me about it.'

I explained my thoughts on Celia's killing and what I needed to know.

Barrow listened and asked some questions. 'Well, Jake, this might be a bit tricky. Firstly, it's a police matter so they should follow this lead. Secondly, it's a military police matter so they should pick it up. Thirdly, it's likely to get bound up in diplomatic niceties with the Afghan authorities and that will bring the diplomatic service into it. Let me just see what we can do.'

It was three days later when Barrow sent for me.

'Okay, Jake, you're going to Afghanistan but you'll be accompanied by a diplomatic bod.'

'Any problems?'

'Not really. The biggest problem was finding Gzifa Sherzai. The police wanted to send Kitty but Gzifa Sherzai wouldn't speak to a woman and wanted to speak to a military person. MI6 said they didn't want to know, so that was a blessing, and the Foreign Office said they must have a person present and the Afghans said they wanted a person present. Anyway, you fly out on British Airways on Tuesday to Karachi and then pick up a flight to Bost Air Field in

Helmand, the only completely civilian airstrip in Southern Afghanistan.'

On the Tuesday morning I received a phone call from Vauxhall Cross, so much for the lack of interest from MI6. That afternoon, with Kitty, I was introduced to my travelling companion. He was a total surprise and it didn't feel right. The meeting was in a block of offices in the West End just off Piccadilly Circus. A very civil servant introduced us to Dan-Dan. Dan-Dan was clearly from the Far East and it turned out his parents were from some hill tribe from a place somewhere in Pakistan that I'd never heard of. No surprise there then. Apparently, he was an expert on Afghanistan and spoke the various languages of the region. Dan-Dan was small, perhaps 5 foot 4 inches with light-brown skin, narrow eyes with epicanthic eyelids and flat expressionless features. His eyes were dead and his voice cold. I saw Kitty give a shudder. The Foreign Office official was charm itself.

'Gentlemen, you probably have been briefed as to what this is about but before we go any further I don't need protection of the sort you appear to be providing,' I said.

Dan-Dan smiled. I supposed it was a smile. 'It takes one to know one, Captain.'

'And we don't need to assassinate anybody.'

Robin Hughes, the Foreign Office guy, appeared aghast. Only a certain class of people are aghast. Normal people are surprised, astonished or even horrified. He was aghast. 'What on earth do you mean, Captain Robinson?' His cultivated voice trembled.

Dan-Dan smiled.

'Who appointed you to this trip, Dan-Dan?' I asked.

'Routine, Captain. You may need an interpreter and you may need protection, so I was given the job.'

'Are you actually an MI6 officer?'

'My status is confidential.'

I turned to Robin Hughes. 'I'll not accept this person as my interpreter. I would prefer somebody else and I believe the highest security needs to be afforded to Gzifa Sherzai. Her location needs to be kept confidential and given only to those who will aid me in talking to her.'

'Captain Robinson, you can't tell us what to do.'

'You're right. I can't. This woman's life is now in your hands. Get it sorted. When you have, contact me again. Good afternoon, gentlemen.'

Kitty and I left.

'I think I know what that was about, but how did you know and are you sure?'

'As the man said, Kitty, "It takes one to know one".'

We returned to the MI5 office and Barrow was waiting. 'A Foreign Office interpreter will join with you when you get to Bost Airfield. He's from the embassy there. He'll also provide transport and security.'

'What about this Dan-Dan guy?'

'What are you talking about?'

I told him about the meeting.

'Right, I see, from now on all contacts will be through me, Jake. It seems like The Family is guarding its arse.'

'Thank you, Barrow.'

That was that then. As I left, Barrow was already on the phone to his MI6 opposite number or it may have been, more likely, the Foreign Office.

26

The trip to Karachi and on to Bost was uneventful. Not just uneventful; it was boring. Barrow had arranged for a diplomatic passport for me and I had a new name: David Devon. I wasn't sure about this and I wasn't sure what my diplomatic role was but clearly somebody thought it a good idea. Customs just waved me through and I was met by a local man, Sebastian James – clearly Oxbridge and a career diplomat – and with him was a local interpreter, Fariad. So Barrow must have talked to the Foreign Office. Fariad was a tall, slim Afghan who spoke perfect English with little accent and had a nice line in cynical humour. I supposed he wore local dress but it seemed there was a fair degree of modification from the traditional clothes. Fariad wore what was known as a shalwar kameez. The kameez was a long shirt, the side seams were open below the waistline and Fariad's one was in a pink colour. The shalwar was a loose pyjama-like pair of trousers that were wide at the top and narrow at the ankle. On his feet he had a pair of pointed, highly polished shoes. He was a mine of information and the few questions I asked him he answered simply and to the point.

There was no air conditioning in the arrivals building and the temperature and humidity were overpowering. As with all new building and systems, nothing was working quite as it should but eventually we ended up with my luggage, mainly due to the insistence of Fariad in his dealings with the airport staff. There was a string of taxis outside the airport and there was also a stand for pre-ordered transport. A taxi with a red rose on the side was waiting there for us. It was a service that the embassy used regularly. Clearly the embassy paid well, as this was a large C-class Mercedes and it had air conditioning. Fariad sat next to the driver, who chattered incessantly about the very uninteresting houses, hovels, humps and hollows in the road that he clearly found fascinating. The only thing that interested me was the quality and range of his English, so I explored it. It appeared that he'd been an illegal immigrant to the UK but decided the weather wasn't to his liking and the roads weren't paved with gold. Social security was not as great as he thought it was going to be, so he came home.

As we pulled away from the airport I noticed another taxi pull out from the rank. The reason I noticed it was that it wasn't near the front of the rank. It too was a Merc. Not a new posh one, though. It was tracking us about 100 yards behind. Perhaps he didn't want to be seen. We pulled into a hotel and I registered. Fariad and Sebastian said they would wait for me while I had a shower and got changed.

My room overlooked the car park, not that it was much of a car park, just a very large barren area with a few parked vehicles. In the far corner was the Merc that had followed us. Sebastian had given me a parcel that I opened in my room. It contained a Glock 17 and a spare magazine. The Glock 17 was a favoured weapon, so Barrow must have briefed the supplier. My personal weapon was a 9 mm SIG P229, but the Glock would do. Clearly, the locals weren't taking chances.

I put on my specially tailored clothes: lightweight, light-blue cotton trousers and white, cotton, short-sleeved shirt. I then put on the shoulder harness that parked the Glock neatly under my left arm. I holstered the weapon and then put on the lightweight sports jacket. It was a beautiful jacket, a Canali. It was fawn with a very faint blue line. This was the sort of sports jacket I'd always wanted and now it had been provided for me and I hadn't even asked for it. The bulge of the gun under my left arm didn't show and the cut of the jacket was such that it hung well, covering any chance of seeing the holster or its strapping with the jacket unbuttoned.

I went down to the lounge. Sebastian was waiting for me and we had a light lunch of Qabili Palau and salad in the dining room. The Qabili Palau was steamed rice mixed with lentils, raisins, carrots and lamb. So it wasn't as light as I assumed it was meant to be. I mentioned the Merc but Sebastian didn't seem perturbed, and informed me that it wasn't additional cover. Looking through the dining room window I could see Fariad sitting on the terrace waiting for us. He was looking towards the Merc. It seemed to me this was let's not worry Jake time.

We left the hotel and the taxi was waiting for us. We drove along the pitted and bumpy road, passing a caravan of camels carrying tents and the household items of a nomad family. They moved steadily but slowly and their loads looked unstable but nothing fell off. I supposed they were looking for grazing land but I didn't ask. Along the roadside were fields of wheat, rice and vegetables. Women and girls were tending the crops and carrying water. They were dressed in brightly coloured Afghan dresses, worn over pants, and chadors, large scarves that are worn over the head. I supposed that was because they were Muslim. There were some men but they didn't seem to be working or appear as colourful as Fariad. The Merc was following us. There was absolutely no doubt and that concerned me. If we weren't the target perhaps Gzifa Sherzai was. We ascended a hill slowly as a herd of about fifteen brown, long-eared goats were wandering in the same direction driven along by two boys. I was tense. This was a good place for a hit. None came. We came over the hill to a crossroads. From the crossroads we took a fine metalled road.

Eventually, we reached the village and it seemed like any other village we had seen, a poor place. We drove very slowly along the road and avoided local pedestrians, who ignored us and wandered aimlessly across our path. The damage from the war was highly visible. There were war-torn buildings and some evidence of rebuilding. It was a pitiable place but set on a rise above the village was an army camp and there were some American soldiers in the village. I supposed that accounted for the new road and a line of small wooden stalls in the centre of the village, a market of sorts. Only the most basic goods seemed to be available. There were several fruit stands and a butcher's shop with slabs of fly-covered meat hanging in the open air. A few shops were selling all sorts of things from batteries to biscuits, sandals to shampoo. We passed a music store that had Persian, Pashto and Hindi tapes on offer. Off to one side was what seemed to be a square of rebuilt shops and more soldiers could be seen there. I supposed that was the upmarket area.

27

We pulled up near a small house, knocked and were invited in. In the living room were three men and a very large woman. It seemed the three men were Gzifa and Muna Sherzai's father, a friend of the family and a local policeman.

Gzifa was fat. Not just plump or large or pleasantly rounded; she was fat. No, she was gross, the next size up from obese. No, two sizes up from obese. She had a fat face with round, rough, dark, ruddy cheeks that welled up in such a way as to make her large, broad, bulbous nose seem small. No, it wasn't small; it was hidden in the fat of her face. Her body was round. Not a nice firm round but a saggy round. A blue loose skirt covered her legs. Her face was uncovered but she wore a scarf covering her hair. The air was polluted by her body odour, an acid, sweaty smell. There are some decisions I wish I'd never made and going there was one of them.

They say that fat people are happy. Well they, the ubiquitous 'they', were wrong when it came to Gzifa. She was miserable. I think she was gross because she was unhappy and unhappy because she was gross.

Introductions were made. Gzifa could speak English and agreed to answer my questions. Unfortunately, I couldn't move my chair any further away from her than it already was.

'Gzifa, I'd be grateful if you could tell me about your

sister, Muna, and the man you knew as Malc and the woman Uzuri.' I thought it would be polite to just see what the woman had to say.

'Uzuri was a friend of my sister. Uzuri was going out with Jason Sergeant Phillips. Her father was in army with Americans.' I assumed he was in the Afghan Army with the Americans or an interpreter. 'My sister say she meet a nice British soldier. I no think that right. Good...'

She asked Fariad something and he translated. 'Well brought up Afghani women shouldn't be friends with foreign soldiers.'

Gzifa then picked up the conversation again. 'It's not, not...' She used an Afghan word.

Fariad, again acting as an interpreter, said, 'Seemly.'

Once again I was impressed with his English. Seemly is not a common word even among native English speakers. They discussed a little more and Gzifa nodded.

'Yes, that right. Not seemly.'

'What was the name of this soldier?' I asked.

'Yes, it the one you say. Malc.'

'Did you meet Malc?'

'Meet him? No, but I see him. He like the other soldiers. He with high soldier who called Major.'

'How do you know the soldier you saw was Malc?'

'Muna tell me. She say Major very important. Malc his friend.'

'Do you know the Major's other names?'

'No, just call him Major.'

'What did he look like?'

'He tall with a smart uniform.'

'What colour was his hair and eyes?'

'He light hair and blue eyes. Muna say he handsome but I not know.'

'Do you know the names of other soldiers?'

'Yes, Jason Sergeant Phillips and one Gil and there one

has name Jibril the angel of the messenger from Allah. The angel revealed the Qur'an to prophet Muhammad. Soldiers of the British not have such a name.'

So that was Gabriel and Gzifa clearly didn't like the idea of a British soldier being called Gabriel.

'Did you see Jibril at any other time?'

'I think yes, but I not sure.'

'Tell me about your sister disappearing.'

'What "disappearing"?'

Fariad answered her and they had a short discussion before Gzifa picked up her story again. 'She say she go to party. I said wrong. Good Muslim girl not go party. She laughed at me. He come in army car.'

'Who came for Muna?'

'I think soldier Malc, but I not know. I not see.'

'You didn't see who was in the car?'

'No, she ran out home, went in car, it went away.'

'She didn't come back?'

'No.'

'What did you do?'

'I tell police. They not help. They say only – how you say? – A bad girl go with soldier and if find her they beat her, she be a, um...' She was hunting for the word and then found it. 'Criminal.'

'What else did you do?'

'I went see Americans. American called liaison. He nice, but he say no can help me.'

'How did you get hold of Sergeant Phillips' email?'

'Email? Yes, Uzuri had email so I send him email but he no reply.'

'Is Uzuri still here?'

'Yes, she work in hospital. She look after children who be hurt. She teacher.'

'Do you think I could talk to her?'

'I think not possible. Her father say she to be married to

man who makes clothes. Her father very angry with British soldiers.'

'Do you think she knows about your sister?'

'I ask her. She very angry. She say Jason Sergeant Phillips, he, um, betrayal her. She say soldier Malc very bad man. He took the heroin and he met with the men who sell opium.'

'How do you know about the heroin and the opium?'

'Humph! You no believe me.'

'I do believe you. I just want more information.'

'Muna, she tell me.'

'So how did she know?'

'I not know.'

'What was the name of the American you saw?'

'He liaison, Captain Gronkowski, I think.'

'Gronkowski?'

'Yes, he gone now to America. But you do nothing. You find soldier Malc, you let him go.'

'What was the relationship between Uzuri and Muna?'

'Relationship?'

'Were they friends.'

'Yes.'

'Did they work together?'

Gzifa looked at Fariad. They had a brief conversation. And he then explained. 'Muna set up the school in the hospital. Uzuri was a nurse and worked in the school. Then Muna disappeared and Uzuri took over running the school.'

'What do you think happened to Muna?' I asked Gzifa. I could see Sebastian shaking his head.

The answer was a surprise. 'I think she dead by British soldiers.'

'Why would they kill her?'

'She know they, they...' She looked at Fariad and they had another short conversation.

Fariad translated. 'Gzifa believes that Malc was making

139

deals for opium and arranging transport to another place. She says that he was doing this for the Major. She says that Sergeant Jason Phillips was working with a lady air force person to fly the opium to somewhere so it can be refined into heroin.'

Gzifa was looking at me. She was bitter, resentful, blaming me and all like me for what was happening in Afghanistan and the loss of her sister. She was crying and her father was comforting her.

It was clear that Gzifa knew very little. I didn't feel she was hiding anything – she wanted information from us that I didn't have – but she had confirmed the drugs trade and who was involved. Altogether a disappointing meeting. I said to Fariad that we should go and he took control with much chatter, nodding and shaking of hands. Gzifa was crying and her father was comforting her and he too was upset. They had lost a family member and I was feeling she was another victim.

As we came out, the Merc that had followed us to the hotel was parked down the road. I had a concern that Gzifa and her relations were in deep trouble and I knew we could do nothing about it.

As we drove away, I went over the information we had, but little of it was factual. Wright was probably a purchaser and user. He was probably with the woman when she disappeared. She could still have been alive but I doubted it. It was unlikely that Gil or Gabriel were involved in the killing but likely involved in drug trafficking. I couldn't help wondering what we would find next. As I tried to stir conclusions in my mind I looked out of the window at the village that lacked electricity or running water, had few cars and scratched a living. I could see no hope that anything we were doing would help these people. As the village disappeared behind us, my loathing for religion and corruption that represses people was reinforced.

28

As we approached the hotel, Sebastian said, 'Your flight isn't until about ten tomorrow. Perhaps you'd like to go for a meal tonight.'

'Thank you, Sebastian. That would be great.'

'It'll be as much business as pleasure. I'd like to introduce you to somebody who may be of value to you in your endeavours to find out what happened to Muna. I'll pick you up at seven thirty,' he told me and left.

It was now two and there's not much to do in an Afghan hotel, even one that supposedly caters for Western businessmen. There was Yasir, the bellboy, who made a suggestion of how I might spend the afternoon mainly by the use of his eyebrows and nods and tilt of his head as the words he used had supposedly innocent meanings. I did what I often did in these situations and started to read my book, a John Grisham, *The Appeal*, and fell asleep.

The creaking of a floorboard woke me. There was somebody in my room and moving slowly and stealthily. The Glock was under my pillow. I slid my hand slowly until I felt the grip and kept my body still. I eased off the safety with my thumb, rolled quickly off the side of the bed, away from the door and swung the gun into the fire position, my elbows on the bed. There was an almighty crash and a squeal of fear.

Yasir, the bellboy, was standing by the low table and around his feet were cups and cakes and a wide variety of goodies and china. He was shaking, he gabbled something, probably in Dari, but it may have been Pashto, the official language and the language of business. His eyes cleared and he tried to speak to me, 'I, I, I.' He got no further.

I put the safety on, pushed the Glock under the pillow and stood up.

'It's okay, Yasir. It's my fault. Let me help you clean this mess up.' He was just delivering afternoon tea, a routine for guests who are in their room in the afternoon.

I picked up a couple of cups and a cake, which I ate.

'No, no, sir, I'll bring fresh, please, please. It's I that am so foolish as to disturb you. Please, sir, please.'

He scurried round the floor and in no time there was no mess and he'd gone, to appear ten minutes later with fresh tea, sandwiches, cakes and bottled water.

After I'd eaten I decided to exercise. I did a simple work out. Push-ups, sit-ups, plank, thrusts, rotations and some others to take the knots out of my muscles and loosen up my joints. I then had a shower and wandered around the hotel grounds. The dusty blue-grey Merc that had been tracking us was across the road. It contained two men and it was making no attempt to hide from me. Was it just checking on me for somebody or was it some sort of pro-tection I'd not been told about, despite the assurance I'd received? There was no way of knowing, so I went back to my room and read.

Later, I got armed and dressed for the evening and wandered down to the bar. I ordered a G and T with ice and lemon, sat at the bar and quietly surveyed the patrons. They were mainly local and wealthy. There were a few foreigners, mainly American as far as I could tell, and I knew I was being watched. I had that creepy feeling that as a kid you get in the dark passageway when going to bed. Of course then there was nobody there but here there was. I sat, sip-ping my drink and watching the people in the lounge. Most just didn't see me as they were bound up in conversations with others in their party and their eyes were locked on to each other, their body movements matching, lifting glasses together, rocking forwards and backwards, hand movements shadowing the movement of another. Some acknowledged me with a nod and brief eye contact and a couple actively ignored me. One was a young woman exposing more leg than is seemly in a Muslim country; the other was a man in his thirties wearing a fawn, single-breasted suit and pale-green shirt with a patterned tie that was mainly brown. What were very noticeable were his polished shoes. I stared at him and eventually he left, which wasn't my intention. I think I embarrassed him. As he left, Sebastian came through the door. He was accompanied by a gorgeous example of womanhood dressed in a delightful cocktail dress, black with red pattern, and clearly a natural blonde. I'm sure every man in the bar looked at her and then at Sebastian with envy. I'm sure every woman in the bar looked at her and wished she looked like that. I slipped off my stool and was about to walk towards them when the young woman, who had been pointedly ignoring me, walked across the floor to Sebastian and his attractive companion. The women hugged, the friendly almost theatrical hug of friends in a closed community. Sebastian then hugged the young woman and kissed her on the cheek. He spoke to her and nodded towards me. They then walked towards me.

Sebastian said, 'Ladies, this is Jake.' He then turned to each of the women in turn. 'This is Claire.' She was the young woman who had been in the lounge. We shook hands. 'And this is Rosemary.' We too shook hands.

'That's just not fair,' I said. They all looked at me, seemingly surprised at what I'd said, and were waiting for an explanation. 'How come he gets a hug and kiss and I don't?'

Rosemary immediately stepped forward and kissed me on the cheek.

'My turn,' said Claire and did the same.

'Would anybody like a drink?' I asked.

'We need to move on,' said Sebastian, taking control.

'Okay,' I said. 'Did you see the man in the fawn suit who left as you came in?'

Sebastian said, 'Yes, but I didn't know him.'

'I saw him,' said Claire. 'He was watching you and pretending he wasn't watching you.'

'Like you were.'

'Well, yes, but I was just hoping you were the Jake that we were going to dinner with.'

'My day has just improved immeasurably or do I have to fight off a retinue of eligible bachelors to have dinner with you?'

'No, you can have me all to yourself, apart from these two, until midnight and then I turn into a wicked witch and fly off on my broomstick.'

Well, that established the pairing.

The large embassy taxi was waiting outside, complete with Fariad, who was now driving. The old Merc that had been parked across the road had gone. Could this all be coincidence?

29

We drove through an area that I couldn't describe as salu-
brious to emerge into an area of fine houses and smart
shops, a few of which were still open. It was very different
from my observations earlier that day. We eventually pulled
up in front of a fashionable-looking restaurant and had no
sooner left the car than we were guided to a table set with
fine linen, silver cutlery and crystal. The clientele around us
looked even more prosperous than those in the hotel. The
walls were hung with exotic rugs and the polished wooden
floor gleamed. Here we had poverty and wealth side by side.
Afghanistan was one of the poorest counties in the world
and yet, among the poverty, there was wealth.

'Tonight,' said Sebastian, 'we're dining on food selected
by Fariad and it seems the chef, Nasir, is delighted by that.'

Nasir, a dignified man who must have been in his late
sixties or early seventies, came and spoke to us. He told us
that the dishes we were going to eat were special occasion
food, the kind eaten at feasts here. He said Afghans don't
eat meals in separate courses but, as a compromise with
Western mores, we were to be served each course separately
at our tables. However, it didn't quite work out like that. It
seemed to me that they just served the food as it was cooked
so we ended up with a number of dishes on the table at the
same time.

I started with ashak, a kind of pasta filled with gandana
that taste a bit like leeks and was anointed with a minty,

145

garlicky, yogurt sauce and savoury minced meat. This description doesn't begin to convey how unusual and delectable a dish it was. The 'pasta' had a slippery lightness, like steamed Chinese dim sum. It went perfectly with the minty flavour of the sauce and the sparing quantity of rich-tasting minced meat. There were also little skewers of lamb kebabs, naan bread, fresh, fragrant, green coriander chutney and an Afghan pilau. I'd eaten numerous rice dishes before, both Eastern and Western, but none had revealed the true delicacy of rice like this one did. There were beautiful heaped platters of zamarud pilau, or 'emerald' pilau coloured with spinach, and qabili pilau, the national dish of Afghanistan, a pilau with lamb, carrots and raisins, perfumed with char masala (a mixture of cloves, cassia, cumin and black cardamom seeds). Another revelation was the shola-e-ghorbandi, the Afghan equivalent of risotto: sticky, short-grained rice cooked with mung beans and yellow split peas and served with a minced lamb and sour plum stew, a haunting mixture of sweet and sour tastes. There was also a delicious okra stew, a buran of fried aubergines served with yogurt and a piquant and refreshing salad, almost like a fresh chutney, made in the true Afghan style from finely chopped tomatoes, cucumber, green chilli, mint and coriander. This was a gastronomic adventure.

Over the meal it turned out that the women worked for the Foreign Office and were on a Middle Eastern learning expedition. They'd been to Saudi and the Yemen, Bahrain and Kuwait, and now they were doing a quick trip in Afghanistan on the way to Pakistan and then home. They chatted away about the adventure it all was. They'd both taken Middle Eastern studies at university and apparently could speak Arabic and Dari but what they were destined for was unclear – as was who they actually worked for, apart from the Foreign Office. It was a whirlwind of conversation, eating, and admiring, and time just flew by.

We left the restaurant and walked round to the car park. Apparently this was odd as the staff normally tip-off the driver and he brings the car round. What was more odd was that there were no staff; they had disappeared into the restaurant. We were alone on the edge of the car park.

'Wait here, we've a problem,' I said. I just knew; the hair on the back of my neck was sending me signals. The car park was empty of cars except for ours at the far end. There was little light and around each hump and bush was a deep, black shadow. I took out the Glock and pushed the safety to fire, walking across the open centre of the car park at a steady pace, not slow and not hurried, scanning for movement as I went. Nothing was moving but it was night and most of the area was dark. The stars twinkled in the clear blue-black sky, pinpoints of light as mysterious as the deep, dark shadows around me. I could smell the dust as it rose from my steps and floated in the air, a dry, acrid smell. There was no breeze, no rustle of leaves, no indicators of movement. I could have been in the sights of a rifle but the air was still silent. Even my companions behind me by the wall of the restaurant were unmoving and now quiet. I could feel the tension as I neared the Merc. Movement? A glimpse out of the corner of my eye. I froze and went down slowly onto one knee, my weapon resting on my left knee. The movement had stopped. I waited. The air was so still and I listened to the silence. Somebody was there but unmoving. For some people stillness is difficult, for me it was a way of life or rather a way to stay alive.

A minute passed. Two minutes. Decision time. I slowly stood and started to move towards the fringe of trees and bushes. A crash. An explosion of movement as somebody crashed through the undergrowth, running away from me. I again went down on one knee and listened to the rush through the bushes and then silence. The bang of a car door, the motor started and it accelerated away. Time to move again. I scanned the periphery. Nothing. Then I moved towards the car. I reached the Merc and took a deep breath to steady my nerves. Fariad was slumped against the steering wheel. I rapidly moved and closed in on the car. The driver's side window was open. I crouched back against the car. It rocked on its springs and I scanned the periphery of the car park. Nothing moved. I stood and looked into the car. Fariad had a black hole at his temple. A trickle of blood had run down his cheek and was now congealed. Gzifa was dead in the back. How she'd died was unclear but it looked to me as if it was torture. Her eyes were open and her face and naked upper body was bruised and mutilated. How she'd been brought here was unknown but the message was clear: stop looking.

I put the Glock to safety and holstered it. If there was someone there intent on killing me they would have tried already but that would have attracted too much attention. Whose attention, though? There was nobody else here.

I joined my companions and told them what I had found. Sebastian was on his mobile phone. This was his territory.

'It would seem your investigating has opened up something that somebody wants hidden,' said Rosemary. So how did she know why I was here and how did she know Gzifa was part of my investigation? These two women weren't what they'd said they were.

'So you two are SIS.'

They looked at Sebastian. 'Ladies, I cannot advise you. It may be that Jake can.'

'Let's go back to my hotel and we can talk.' We stood in uncomfortable silence for the next ten minutes and the local police arrived. Sebastian spoke to them and they unhappily took the two bodies away and the Merc. If there had been any forensic evidence their lack of any systematic process or precautions would have certainly destroyed it. Eventually, a taxi arrived and took us back to the hotel.

'Okay, ladies, I'll show you mine then I expect you to show me yours.'

They smiled and agreed. I told them what we had on the murders and who was involved.

Rosemary was the spokesperson. It turned out they were both SIS operational officers. Rosemary was from a counter-terrorism team and was a case officer. Her job was covert intelligence operations. She had a number of local people giving her information. She'd built a picture of a particular drugs operation that was being used to fund a terrorist group targeted at the UK. Claire, on the other hand, worked in London. She was a targeting officer. Her job was to analyse the information gathered from a variety of sources and use her analytical skills to build up intelligence pictures of the area of interest and contribute to operational planning. It was my intervention into Afghanistan that caused her to come here. I fed them everything I had and something seemed to be ringing bells for them but in general terms we were on parallel tracks and unlikely to join up. I agreed that I'd feed them all the information we gathered but they couldn't give me the same assurance.

I was ready to go home, only a little wiser than when I came. One of the real problems in life is that if you don't really know what you're looking for you're unlikely to find it. However, what the trip had done was confirm a number of suspicions.

30

It was morning and Sam had gone to work. It was London and it wasn't raining. Now that had to be an unusual experience. My mobile rang; it was Kitty. Her message was simple:

'We'll pick you up at Arnos Grove Station in half an hour. We know where Wright is.'

Now that's the beauty of working with the Met CID. London has millions of people in millions of houses in thousands of roads yet because of their network they can find people. It's not easy but they can do it.

I walked out of the station and the car was there. Gaygan was chatting to a traffic warden, probably because he was on a double yellow line, but it was clearly a friendly chat. I slipped into the back of the car. Gaygan got into the driver's seat and we pulled smoothly away from the kerb into the stream of traffic and along Oakleigh Road South. We pulled over.

Kitty turned in her seat to face me and said, 'He'll be coming down there in about five minutes. You wait here. If he runs it may be in this direction. We'll be behind him.' She pointed up the road in the direction we'd been travelling. 'So if he goes that way we'll get him. Are you clear?'

'Yes, ma'am. Crystal.' I sat up straight with my arms folded with raised elbows.

'Oh, piss off!' She smiled.

I got out of the car and watched it travel up the road. It

stopped and both Kitty and Gaygan got out. I lounged against a wall merging into the scenery.

A figure came down the steps of a house and turned towards me. He wasn't hurrying, just ambling. No, it was an unsteady, ungainly shuffle. He was wearing an army great-coat that had seen better days and a black woolly beanie. One trouser leg was tucked into his sock like he was going to ride a bike. Was he carrying? His head was down and shoulders hunched. I just waited. He did not appear to have noticed me. When he was three paces away from me, I stepped out into the centre of the pavement. The move-ment alerted him. He looked up, saw me, turned, took one step away not looking where he was going and ran slap bang into Gaygan who was a couple of paces behind him.

Clink, clunk, the cuffs went on and Gaygan led him to the car. Kitty was already in the front passenger seat. Gaygan put Wright in the rear, nearside backseat and fitted his seatbelt. I went round the other side of the car and got in. Gaygan got in behind the wheel, started the car and the doors clunked as the locks slipped home. Up to that point I'm convinced that nobody said anything. Wright just slumped in his seat and seemed to go to sleep.

We were heading for the Earls Court Road where Kitty was stationed and the smell increased at each junction and traffic manoeuvre as the car lurched and Wright rocked. I put down the windows. It made little difference to the polluted atmosphere. It was clear that he was drugged up to the eyeballs. When we arrived, we led Wright to a cell and Kitty sent for a doctor or FME as she called him, but who turned out to be a 'her' and she was a local GP. Before she arrived Wright was searched. His trouser leg was full of little self-sealing clear plastic bags of what we assumed to be heroin as it had the brown colour. He would be done for possession at the minimum and probably supplying. A local detective sergeant would handle that but Kitty had priority.

151

He was stripped, his soiled clothes were put into black plastic bags and he was dressed in a paper suit. The FME declared that Wright was unfit to be interviewed and would need at least six hours to fully recover from the mix of drugs and alcohol he'd consumed. She recommended we take him to the local hospital and she sent for an ambulance. Not only was he saturated with narcotics and alcohol, he also had a number of physical injuries that needed treatment and she wanted an x-ray of his hands and ribs. It seemed that Wright had been involved in a serious fight, probably a couple of days before. I might have known, seeing the state of his face. He had two vicious scratches down his right cheek, one of which was infected and the other was healing but they could have been the result of the fight. So that was that then; we were to be on standby until the evening.

31

I switched on my phone to find I had a message to ring the Wicked Witch of the West, so I rang her. Having a spell cast on me was the last thing I wanted. Vera answered in her normal abrupt, efficient way, but when she found out it was me she softened. How strange! She was almost sympathetic. She wanted me to see Sir Nicolas as soon as possible, so I set off straight away. There was nothing I could do at Earls Court.

I walked into the reception of the chambers to be confronted by a vision of loveliness but it wasn't Sam.

'Can I help you, sir?'

'I'm Jake Robinson and I'm going up to see Sir Nicolas.'

'Would you like to take a seat, sir?'

'Who are you?'

'I'm Gillian, sir, and–'

'I'm Jake. Good morning, Gill. I'll see you when I come down.'

I headed for the lift. 'The name is Gillian, sir.' Her voice was prissy.

'Yes, I heard and I bet you reserve Gill only for men who have slept with you.' Her mouth fell open and the door of the lift shut before she recovered.

As I stepped from the lift into Sir Nicolas's outer office Vera was on the phone.

'It's all right, Gillian. Jake works here and has an important meeting with Sir Nicolas.' There was a pause.

Vera was nodding. 'Yes, Gillian, I'll have a word with him about that.' She put down the phone and turned towards me.

I held my hands held up in surrender. 'I'll apologise when I go down, Vera.'

'I know you will, Jake.' She was accepting, almost forlorn. Her head was down. There was something very wrong. This definitely wasn't the Wicked Witch of the West that I'd come to admire. She was dejected. 'Please go straight in, Jake.' There was a catch in her throat; she didn't look at me.

As I walked in, Sir Nicolas rose, walked over to me, took my elbow and led me to the table where we normally sat. Now I knew there was something seriously wrong. He handed me an envelope then went to the window and looked out. He was totally still. On the envelope it just said *Jake*. I opened it and started to read the letter.

My Dearest Jake,
I never believed I would ever write this letter but there are things I've not told you. I'm married. That may come as a shock to you. I had a secret and I knew that secrets would eventually drive us apart. As time went on my feelings for you became deeper, and the deeper they became the harder it became to tell you my secret. I wrote to my husband, we talked and to my surprise, shock really, he wants me back. I faced a dilemma. I had to choose. The choice was not him or you, it was him and my children or you. I have two girls. I want you and I want my girls but as things are I can't have both. I realised last night that I had to give them up or give you up. I couldn't dump you with this problem and the complexities I'm faced with, so I've flown away to join my children.

I have a great fear that I'll live to regret this decision but by then it will be too late to recover, so goodbye my lover. Goodbye to the most wonderful man I've ever been lucky enough to meet.

Perhaps you would be much better off with a yellow rubber duck than me. See, I can even mimic your little jokes.

I'll always love you and I'll bring up my children to model my lost love.

Sam

My whole body was cold, freezing, I was shivering. It was like I was ten again when I fell through the ice on the village pond. Not fear, just lost, didn't know what to do, abandoned. I looked up. Sir Nicolas came and sat at the table looking at me. I could feel the tears in my eyes. I was so in love with Sam. I never even saw this coming or perhaps I wasn't in love with her enough to see it coming. There I go again, analysing the un-analysable. The room was silent. I couldn't feel my feet and my hands were numb. I was having difficulty breathing. This was the worst thing that had ever happened to me. I felt the tears on my cheeks. I reached in my jacket for my SIG. Sir Nicolas reached across and caught my wrist and shook his head. I let go of my SIG. He was right.

He spoke. 'Vera cried this morning. I've never seen Vera cry before. Over thirty years and I'd never seen her cry before. She just loved watching you and Samantha spar when you joined us. She just loved it when you two got together. I think she saw it as the love match that she never had and could never have so she was living it through you two. When Samantha came and spoke to us this morning Vera was shattered. For what it's worth, Jake, I couldn't see how Samantha could overcome the problems she faced. The reality is she cannot divorce and if she didn't return she couldn't see her children. If she did return she couldn't leave again and there is always the risk that they will kill her.' He paused, took a deep breath, inflating his cheeks, and blew out through pursed lips. This was the most balanced, controlled man I had ever met but he was emotional. He was fighting off the tears. He shook his head. 'You're a tough loner, Jake; you'll survive anything. Would you like some coffee?'

He hadn't paused between the last two statements, very un-Sir Nicolas like. When in doubt have some coffee or a nice cup of tea. That's the very English solution to the world's problems.

The door opened and Grace came in with the coffee. Vera's witch's telepathy must have been working. Grace didn't ask, she just served. She left. No smile, and no flutter of the eyelids.

'Why, sir? Why?'

'Sam married a Muslim. I suppose he bought her really – multi-millionaire, palace, servants, the whole bit. I represented him in some matters. He's older than Sam. We all do daft things when we're young. When she left him she came to me and then you turned up. So different in so many ways and she was as smitten as you were. Jake, there'll be no going back. I'm surprised she's alive. If she'd been of his nationality his family would have killed her already.'

I heard his warning and noticed he gave me no information. I'd never know where she was and if I did find out it was clear that she would be killed or I would.

'What will you do now, Jake?' asked Sir Nicolas.

That was a simple question with a simple answer. 'I'm going to buy a rubber duck, a yellow one, then I'm going home to sit in the bath with my rubber duck and sort myself out.'

He smiled and shook his head while looking at me with friendly eyes.

'I think you should cut away and do that now then.'

When I reached the ground floor, I spied Gillian. She was dealing with a client so I waited. I went up to her and apologised. She accepted my apology and I left and went home to an empty flat, complete with my brand new, yellow rubber duck that cost me 50p. I'm a hard man or so it has been said, but I didn't think so and right then I was a shattered man, so I had a bath with my yellow duck called Sam and then went to bed. Tomorrow was going to be a new day and a new life. The past had gone. I had friends who had left me, mainly because they died – no, mainly because they'd been killed – and that finality was easier than this, but life goes on. Only one person had ever lingered with me and that was Frances and I suppose that was because I visited her grave regularly. Daft really, but it helped my thinking. Then Sam came along and she became my life. I thought about her when I was breathing in and when I was breathing out. She was the last thing on my mind when I went to sleep and the first thing when I woke up in the morning. Well, that life had ended. Nowhere to visit, I just had a rubber duck. Rubber ducks don't have secrets and they don't leave you. But a new life starts tomorrow. Yes, Pauline the psychiatrist was right, I was made for this life, self-sufficient and not really expecting to live long enough to get old. In fact, living to an old age was my biggest fear. No, second biggest fear. The greatest fear was that I would die slowly.

32

That evening, I phoned Kitty and told her that I needed to take a few days off.

'You bloody can't, Jake. We need you. Wright is being difficult and only you can handle it.' She knew and I knew she could handle any and all questioning of suspects.

'Come on, Kitty. I need a break.'

'And we need you here.' There was something in her voice. She knew and I bet it was Barrow who had spoken to her. Sir Nicolas would have spoken to him. 'Please, Jake.' I couldn't interpret the tone in her voice, but it was a mix of things. Was it sympathy? Kitty didn't do sympathy but the need was there.

But I knew deep down that I couldn't stay at home any-way. What the hell would I do apart from just get more miserable or drunk, or miserable *and* drunk? 'Okay, I'm on my way.' I put down the phone and got dressed.

When I arrived at the police station I was met with a surprise. Malcolm Wright would only talk to me, so I went in to see him. He had been cleaned up, dressed in one of those overall suits that the police use when they take your clothes, and he didn't smell. He seemed quite balanced, must be on methadone.

'Captain, I don't want a lawyer; I want you as a prisoner's friend.'

This was all I needed. I didn't want to be anybody's friend and particularly not someone like Wright.

'I'm not sure that can be done. You should have a solicitor.'

'I just want an advisor.'

'Yes, I understand what you want but you can't have what you want. You can, however, have a solicitor free of charge. I'm neither qualified nor am I acceptable as your counsel in this situation.'

'Supposing I decide not to have a solicitor. What would you advise me to do when they question me?'

I just wanted to tell him to fuck off but I must have been going soft. 'Be very clear about what question you're being asked. If you're not quite sure, specify what you think the question is in your own words and then just answer that question. If you're asked an open question, such as what happened on the morning of so and so, ask them to be more specific. Only ever tell them the truth. If you're asked a question you don't want to answer just say "no comment".'

'Will you be questioning me, Captain?'

'No. The police will interview you.'

Kitty and Gaygan interviewed Malcolm Wright. They did everything by the book and I just observed. Gaygan started off with the easy ones – What is your name? How do you know Major Carmichael? – and established the basic information that they knew already. He made it clear that this was to do with the murder of Jason Phillips, drugs and the murder of some women. He would be questioned under caution but could leave at any time and have a solicitor. The drugs charge would be treated separately.

Kitty said, 'I want to ask you some questions about where you've been recently. Is that all right?'

'I suppose.'

'Tell me the towns you were in in July.'

'I was here in London of course. I went down to Brighton and I went to Exeter.'

159

'Why did you go to Brighton?'

'You're gonna laugh. I met this bird in Streatham. I promised her a day out in Brighton if...well, you know. So we did the deed and I took her to Brighton. We had a great day, went on the pier, had hot doughnuts, went on the bumpers and behaved like a couple of kids. Course we were as high as kites most of the time on coke, but it was the best day out I'd had in years.'

'Have you seen her again?'.

'No, well, she's married an everythin'. Works in some council job.'

'It sounds like you had a good time. What about Exeter?'

'Oh, that was a cock up.'

'What happened?'

'Nothing.'

'Why did you go to Exeter?'

'Well, it was Holty.'

'You mean Gabriel Holt?'

'Yeah. He gave me a ring and said he was goin' down there and he'd a contact that could get a supply of blow. Sounded good so I went. I got down there and got another call what said the meet had bin changed to some place called Heartlybridge. Bugger that. I'd come down all that way by train. Cost a bleedin' fortune. I wasn't gonna bugger about finding some other hick place I'd never heard of. I had a few jars had a few laughs in a couple of pubs and went home.'

'If you'd gone by car would you have gone to Heartlybridge?'

'Probably, but gettin' trains is a pain.'

'Do you read the newspapers?'

'Course. Sometimes.'

'When you read them what do you read?'

'The football and the racin'.'

'Have you read about any crimes recently?'

'S'pose.'

'Tell me about any of them.'

'Christ, I don't remember them.'

'So you don't remember a murder near Heartlybridge?'

'Now, just hang on a bit. I don't murder people. Is that what this shit is all about?'

'Partly.'

'Well, you can partly fuck off.'

'Tell me about Major Carmichael.'

'No comment.'

'Why no comment?'

'Look, I didn't kill him neither.'

'No, we know that but you were his friend.'

'Who bloody told you that?'

'Well, you went to America with him.'

'Yeah, so what?'

'What was that all about?'

'Oh, he was goin' to get some job with the Americans. An' we just went with him.'

'Who are we?'

'Holty an' me.'

'Why did Gabriel Holt and you go with Major Carmichael?'

'Well him and Holty had a thing.'

'A thing?'

'Yes, well, they were a pair of poofs and they were in love. Stupid bastards. They were always at it. I'm surprised they didn't get caught.'

'But you're not a poof?'

'Christ, no! Straight as a die, me.'

'So why did you go?'

'No comment.'

'So you *are* a poof.'

'No, I'm not.'

'Then why did you go with them?'

'Business, weren't it?'

'Business?'

'Yeah, with that Susan bird from the RAF.'

'Susan Thomas?'

'Yeah.'

'So, you were doing her then.'

'Christ, you got sex on the brain. Mind you, I bet she'd be a goer.'

'Well, what business then?'

'I suppose now the major's dead it don't matter. They were into drugs in a big way. I just ran messages and collected stuff and things.'

'Was anyone else involved?'

'Course.'

'Who?'

'Jase.'

'Jason Phillips.'

'He was more than involved; he ran the whole bloody thing. Bloody look at me I'm a hero Carmichael was nothing really. Jase was the man.'

'You're saying that Jason Phillips was the brains behind the drug smuggling.'

'Yeah and he was doin' Susie-bloody-smarty-knickers.'

'By that you mean he was having sexual intercourse with her.'

'Oow, sexual intercourse. Now there's posh. He'd have a bird's knickers off before they realised it.'

'So, he'd had lots of relationships?'

'Are you into porn then, Inspector?' He grinned at her with his head on one side. 'I don't fink you'd make a million.'

Kitty gave him a friendly smile. 'You're probably right. I'm just surprised that Jase was a ladies' man.'

Kitty was playing this beautifully. She was just letting him take her along and building on what he said.

162

'Yeah, the one-night stand man. But he could stand all night if you know what I mean.'

'So he just picked girls up?'

'No, he liked them rich – posh birds looking for a bit of rough.'

'Only one-night stands?'

'Oh no. He'd a couple of regulars, like Susie-blue-knickers. They were posh birds as well but not from toff families, if you know what I mean. He just done the toff birds to get his own back.'

'I don't understand. Get his own back?'

'Well, it seems his mum was a rich bird and stuck him in a home. So he said he'd shag them all and I think if he hadn't ended up in the clink he would have done.'

'Can you remember any of their names?'

'Give over!'

'Did he have any rich birds in Iraq?'

'Christ, you got the hots or sumink? Yea, he did and in Afghanistan. Don't know how he did it. Nobody was getting local totty, yet he was getting posh local totty. He got this doctor, in Baghdad. Sort of specialist kids doctor. Went on for about a week that one before he dumped her.'

'She was a paediatrician then?'

'Yeah, that's right. Was sort of English but also Iraqi.'

'You know any in the UK?'

'No, not really. He'd one he met at a dojo or something like that. I think it was a judo place.'

'Were there any that were dancers?'

'Oh yeah, at least three. He had them on the go at the same time then – wham! – he moved on.'

'What sort of dancing?'

'Christ, I don't know. Sorta jiggin' round the floor together sort of dancing. They were teaching people and into competitions an' stuff.'

'Did Gabriel Holt or the major know about this?'

'Christ, no! They were too busy shagging each other to see what Jase was doing.'

'I bet you're hungry with all that talking. Let's get you some food. Then I want to show you some photos to see if you recognise some women.'

33

While Malcolm Wright went to the canteen with Gaygan, Kitty and I laid out an arrangement of photos. We drew a selection of women who looked to be in the correct age bracket and were attractive. Among them we mixed photos of the murdered women and a couple of women that we knew went out with Jason Phillips who we believed were alive. That morning, Morgan Jones, the police artist, had set up an easel and his stick of charcoal slipped across the paper drawing fine lines. As far as I could see, the lines had no relationship to the photo of the dead face on the mortuary photo. Then, with a blackened finger and concentrated thought, he smudged the lines and the face emerged. More lines, more smudges and there was a sketch of the person in the photo looking more alive than the photos of live people. Five times he worked his magic and we had five lifelike sketches of five dead people, two who were listed murder victims. He set up each picture in a frame, jiggled with some lights, took some photos, ran his computer and we had a complete set of pictures of murdered women and three pictures of other dead women. Throughout this process he said not one word and on completion, handed me the pictures, smiled, inclined his head at my thanks then collected his paraphernalia and left.

When Wright came back into the room where the photo sheets were on the table, Kitty asked if he could identify any of the women. We were in luck.

'I recognise her,' said Wright. 'She was at the dance place but Jase didn't go out with her. She was the boss lady.'

He'd identified Claire Forest, the professional ballroom dancer.

'Can you tell us anything about her?'

'Not really.'

'Where did you see her?'

'I reckon she brought round – what's her name? Funny name – I know, Adonella. No, but it was like that. I know, it was Andonella.'

'You don't know her last name do you?'

'Nah.'

'Do you know the name of this woman?' Kitty was pointing at the identified photo of the professional dancer, Claire Forest.

'No, I only saw her a couple of times and never spoke to her.'

Malcolm then identified two Iraqi women and he knew their names Ghadah Qasim and Maali Mizher, although his pronunciation was way off beam.

'Did you know any other women in Iraq who went out with Jase?'

'Well sort of. There was an American who was from an Iraqi family. I think her name was something like Rababa. We called her Rabbits.'

'What did she do?'

'She worked in the legal office and translated stuff. I think she was a lawyer.'

'You said, "sort of went out with her"?'

'Well, she was married to a colonel.'

'British or American?'

'American.'

'And sort of went out?'

'It was funny really. I think he really fancied her. She wasn't just nookie. I think she went back to the States.'

'Do you know where?'

'Not sure, but she was in Washington when we were there.'

'Did Jase see her?'

'Course! That's how I know she was there.'

'So we've a female lawyer of Iraqi descent married to an American colonel who served in Iraq.'

'S'pose.'

'Any others that you recognise?'

'Her.' He was pointing at Vikki Coombes.

'Where did you see her?'

'Well, I didn't actually see her.'

'So how did you recognise her?'

'Well, it was sort of a joke really. She was on a photo leading a small horse with a little kid on it. Jase said that he and some bird was at a horse trial thing and this bird' – he pointed at the photo – 'came into the place where they get off and the horse was all sweaty. Jase told this bird that her horse is sweating a bit and she said, "If you'd been doing what this horse has been doing between my legs for the last quarter of an hour you'd be sweating too". Jase laughed and this bird got all embarrassed and rode off.'

Both Kitty and Gaygan were laughing.

'Jase was good with stories like that.'

'What was the name of the woman that Jase was seeing at the horse trial?'

'Katy Ravioli.'

'Could that be Katherine Ravillious?' I asked.

'Yeah that's it. She was something else. Her dad was some sort of banker. Greek or something.'

Kitty looked at me with a question in her eyes. We knew Katherine Ravillious apparently eloped with some garage mechanic. Her father had offered half a million for any information that might lead to finding her, but she never turned up.

167

That was the last of the people that Malcolm Wright could recognise.

'One more thing, Malcolm,' I asked. 'Do you remember a woman named Muna Sherzai?'

'No, well, ah hmm. I don't think so.' He turned his head to the left and looked down as he answered, avoiding eye contact. Clearly, the question had shaken him.

'Okay, Malc. Oh, about the drugs business, were there any Americans involved?'

'Yeah, course.'

'Many?'

'Quite a few.'

'Can you remember any names?'

'There was this guy name Hank Yarfield. Yeah, Geoffrey Theaston. He was an artist or sumfink, and another one, an officer name Gronkowski.'

'Gronkowski. That doesn't sound very American.'

'No, suppose not, but he had lots of local contacts.'

'Thank you, Malc.'

Kitty bailed Wright to appear in a couple of days and had him driven home. Now the hunt was on for the people who had been identified, but as far as we knew were alive.

Gaygan wrote the information we had on the board.

Known Iraqis dead and friends of Jason Phillips
- *Ghadah Qasim worked with Mary Telford*
- *Maali Mizher*

To check on: Rababa somebody, nicknamed Rabbits. American lawyer or legal secretary married to an American colonel in Iraq and returned to the USA, Washington?

Dead in UK
- *Vikki Coombes – Horsey*
- *Celeste Biever – Horsey*
- *Linda Geddes – Judo 7th Dan*
- *Claire Forest – Ballroom champion*

Missing, suspected murdered
- *Andonella Thomson – Dancer*
- *Katherine Ravillious – Daughter of a banker*

Murdered RMP Corp – Celia Foley ??
Missing in Afghanistan – Muna Sherzai
Other murders that may be related
- *Sgt J Billinghurst*
- *Mary Telford*

Attempted Murder
- *Jake Robinson*

The three of us sat and looked at the board.

'Can I sum up and say what I think?'

The other two nodded.

'I believe Malcolm Wright carried out all the murders except for Celia Foley. I think that was either Wright or Holt. I think we need to talk to a trusted psychiatrist who may give us a clue but the why isn't really important, yet. We've a profile of the murdered women, but I've a feeling that there are some women who don't fit the profile who have been murdered but their bodies haven't been found, and the way they were killed may be different as may be the disposal of the bodies.'

The other two were looking at me. I had the impression that they disagreed but they didn't contradict me.

'Let me come back to Celia. I believe that Gabriel Holt or Malcolm Wright killed Celia Foley. The reason was that Gabriel was in love with Carmichael and he feared that Carmichael would be blamed for the murders. I think he believes Carmichael carried out the murders. He thought Celia had information so he tortured her and then finished the job with a copycat killing. The question here is how did he know the pattern of the original killings? I can't think why Malcolm Wright might have killed Celia. Susan Thomas probably knows about Jason Phillips and if she does she could be a witness. Odd question: why did Randolph Mabry want to find Jase's killer?'

'Jake, why don't you go home and let us think about what you've said and come up with a plan?'

She must have had a call from Barrow or Sir Nicolas. Don't argue, Jake. Just go home. So I did.

34

The next morning I visited Frances's grave and sat on the bench. I was lost and alone so I told Frances. I hadn't eaten; I had a gnawing emptiness in my stomach and the same feeling in my head. The clouds were building up and threatening rain. That was all I needed. I knew Frances was listening and sympathising, but she was telling me to be strong and to focus on the job, so I did. We had Josey's list of names and the initials next to them, so I asked Frances and she told me I was an idiot. I pulled out the list from my wallet. The initials were the dead women and the names were Jase's girlfriends. G Q / Forogh Hatf, MM / Hadiya Khan, VC / Michelle Goldman, CB / Joan Jones, LG / Lesley Marshal, CF / Phyllis Smith, AT / Gill Lake, KR / Ann Palmer. So KR was Katherine Ravillious and Jase went out with Ann Palmer. It was so obvious, sitting there on my own, talking to Frances. If anybody knew what I was doing they would have locked me up. I wanted to cry, so I laughed. 'They're coming to take me away ha haa!' I often wondered if other people have dead people they talk to. The only question remaining was about the links between the murdered women whose initials we had and Jase's girlfriends. I knew I knew the answer to that. The pain in my stomach and in my head disappeared. The sun broke through the clouds and I knew what I had been seeing and feeling was my own misery. I would be fine now. I had a suspicion that Jase's girlfriends worked for the murdered women. I suppose the clue was that Linda Geddes – judo seventh dan – had trained Lesley Marshal, judo lightweight champion who had a relationship with Jase. A plan was equally obvious; find these women.

'Good morning, Captain Robinson,' a voice from behind me said. The accent was American. I turned and the woman who owned it looked Middle Eastern.

'Good morning. You know me?'

'I was at Jason Phillip's trials. I saw you at the first one but you weren't at the second one. Oh, you don't know me. I'm Rababa McDaniel.'

'They called you Rabbits.'

'Yes, that's correct.'

'You know about Jase?'

'That he's dead, yes.'

'And you came looking for me?'

'Well, yes. Sort of.'

'Sort of?' I paused, waited. 'How can I help?'

'Can I sit down?' I nodded. She sat next to me. 'A friend of yours?' She nodded towards the grave.

'Yes. She was my boss. Her name's Frances. She was killed.'

'You were close?'

'We spent a lot of time together. I come and talk to her when I've got a problem.'

Rababa smiled. 'It's good to have someone to talk to.' She was staring at me. 'He didn't kill Maali Mizher or Ghadah Qasim, you know.'

'Who did?'

'It wasn't Jase.'

'I know that; I just don't know who did it.'

'It could only have been one of three people.'

'Go on.'

'Malcolm Wright, Gabriel Holt or that bastard Carmichael, but I think it was Malcolm Wright.'

'Why?'

'They came over to Washington. Carmichael and Gabriel were, you know, gay and were together all the time, but Wright was always on the prowl.'

'But why do you think he would be a killer?'

'Oh, I don't know. Just a feeling.'

'You didn't look me up just to tell me Jase wasn't a killer.'

'No.' She sounded uncertain. 'Well, yes I did.'

'How did you find me?'

'I asked Gabriel and he told me where you lived. I followed you and you came here.'

'Go back home, Rababa. Remember Jase as he was and he wasn't a serial killer.'

She smiled. 'Thank you, Captain Robinson. Thank you.' There was a sob in her voice, tears in her eyes and I could feel the relief in her tone. We stood and she threw her arms around me and kissed me on the cheek. 'Thank you, oh thank you.' There was a break in her voice and the tears ran down her cheeks, but they were tears of joy. It felt great to bring some happiness into somebody's day. She then walked away, straight-backed, and just looked straight ahead. I was sure she was crying but I didn't know. What I was clear about now was that Jase went with a number of women and they were the people he dated over a period of a couple of years. Josey had collected those names and she was checking out the dead women, so next to Jase's girlfriend's names were the dead women's initials. What I wasn't yet positive about was the relationship between the girlfriends and the murdered women.

The picture for me was clearer – well, a bit like a modern art picture; you know what it is even if the whole thing is a bit muddled but the problem can be that if you look at it in a different light what you see can change, so I fixed the image.

I phoned Kitty. She was at the factory. 'I'm coming in, Kitty, and can I borrow Gaygan?'

'What for?'

'That list of names and initials; the names are Jase's partners and the initials are the dead women. I want Gaygan to find the partners and talk to them. Well find out whether Wright was banging the dead women.'

'Okay and how is he going to do that?'

'Let me think. Oh yes, he'll have to use standard hard work using the police national database, national archives, electoral rolls, 192.com, etc. You know, standard bloody hard boring work but when he's found them he can do the interviews.'

I went into the station and sat down with Gaygan. I gave him the list and he told me how he was going to tackle the problem. Three days later, we hit pay dirt. Gaygan had reported to Kitty that he'd conducted three interviews. He had very strong indications that Wright was our man and he would press on. He'd tied up two missing persons with two women that Jase had had a relationship with: Linda Mercer, who was an HR Director, and Penny Allan, the owner of a boutique. The two women he interviewed were Debbie Carter, an HR officer, and Louise Bennett, a sales assistant. Apparently, they still had very fond memories of Jase. Now the picture was clearer, so Gaygan and I sat down with Kitty. Gaygan outlined what he'd found. He had six missing women who satisfied the criteria and he had their job addresses, all of which were on the database. He then located women who knew them and put feelers out about Jase, and – bingo! – these two came up.

'So, Kitty we have a pattern. Well, the indication of a pattern,' I said.

'So, missing people have friends and these two worked with them. I'm not sure about the significance of what you can see, Jake.'

'The women I interviewed,' said Gaygan, 'who went out with Jase, worked for the missing women.'

'And that tells us what?' Kitty couldn't see it.

'It gives us motive, Kitty,' I said.

'Um, how?' asked Kitty.

'We're dealing with a serial killer. That, almost by definition, means we're dealing with a sociopath. We're looking for somebody who is or was targeting the boss or superior to the woman whom Jase had had relationships with. Jase is the new moon. When he comes out the woman's boss is for the chop.'

'So, it could be Jase?'

'Yes, but I don't think so. It's somebody who wants to feel superior to Jase, so they go up a level. If Jase has a corporal as a girlfriend her sergeant is in the frame for killing if the sergeant is a female.'

Kitty just sat looking at me, thinking. 'It has to be Wright, doesn't it?'

I didn't confirm or deny this line, but continued my musing. 'This all fits, apart from Celia. Jase didn't sleep with anybody who reported to her. She was the first level. Josey would have been the target.'

'But Josey was dead.'

'So we've the exception that proves the rule or her killing was for a different reason and that reason lies in the torture.'

'For information?'

'I reckon, Kitty.'

'So Celia's killer could be Wright and Holt.'

'Why, Kitty?' This was my view but I wanted her reasoning.

'For information. Holt wants to clear his lover's name.'

'I think we're all systems go, Kitty.'

35

Kitty rang me that evening and told me that they were burying Celia Foley the following afternoon at Amesbury in Wiltshire. I thought it odd as she didn't come from that area but apparently that's where she wanted to be buried. I wondered about things like that. I hadn't decided where I wanted to be buried and if I had I suppose I would have put it in my will, that's if I had a will, which I didn't. We drove down. It was an easy journey down the M3 then the A303.

Josey was buried in the same cemetery. Odd the way things turn out. I'd missed Josey's funeral; well, I didn't know she was dead until after she was buried, so, as I had the opportunity, I visited her grave but she wouldn't know.

The cemetery, like many, was flat, bare, cold and stretched out to the side and back of the bleak, grey, stone Saxon church, with high-set windows looking down with dead eyes on the headstones. No trees to give it life, just rows of gravestones, cold, grey, granite and slate, lighter limestone and some marble gravestones, many complete with wilted cut flowers and there were even cheap cast concrete ones, a poor remembrance for a life. I'd never quite worked out why bodies are buried. Cremation was for me a much better option. I can remember talking to a woman in the funeral business once. I suggested that as graves were so large as people are buried flat, they could instead be put into tubes and dropped into holes drilled in the ground. She said that was being done already but I

176

hadn't seen it. There again, I'm not a frequent attendee at funerals or cemeteries. No, that wasn't true; I visited Frances regularly.

I found Josey's grave in the bleak field of gravestones. It had a simple granite cross with her name, rank, date of birth and date of death on it. No loving memorials, no hearts and roses, no verses, just plain words on a basic cross. Still, she had a headstone. I wondered who paid for it; she had no family if I remembered rightly. Perhaps it was Celia.

I've never known what closure was. A limitation on my emotional education, I suppose. I asked somebody in the funeral business once. He said there's nothing simple about the death of a loved one. He said perhaps there's a loved one in your life who has passed away, but you find yourself continuing to think about them. He said it was important for my health physically, mentally and emotionally that I find a way to move on with my life. I suppose he was right. Perhaps a funeral is part of that or some ceremony at which you accept they have gone and that you loved them and it's not your fault. I suppose that's why I go and talk to Frances and why I had to visit Josey's grave. These people were important to me and I had to say goodbye when they went. I suppose, perhaps, Sam will never leave me. I suppose I could have been upset that she chose her children over me but that would just have been selfish. I was just going to have to begin a new chapter in my life. But it would be tough. I knew I was never going to forget her and didn't really even want to do that. I just wanted her back, but being realistic that wasn't going to happen. I could always live in hope but if I did I would never move on. My memories would always be there inside of me but I needed to get on with my life. We come into this world with nothing and most of us go out with not much more, but it would be nice to be missed. I remember an army padre saying that when we're born our hands are open and empty to receive God's love and when we die our hands are closed and empty as we passed on all we are to those we love. I'm not sure that's altogether true though. Not that death concerns me much. If I dropped dead now I wouldn't know so why worry about it? Still, Josey's killer was also dead and I was alive and had a funeral to observe.

I watched the mourners gather. Mum and Dad were clearly identifiable and two girls had the same plump build as Celia and were the same sort of age, so they were probably sisters. There were about a dozen people altogether and they looked like they belonged. Nobody was out of place.

There is the idea that killers, particularly those that torture their victims, turn up at the funeral to get closure. Mind you, if they were the cause perhaps they were seeking some sort of absolution. No, people do say such stupid things.

Kitty and Gaygan were watching the gate of the cemetery. I was the man on the spot and the only one out of place. My earpiece crackled. It was Kitty.

'We've a visitor, Jake. The man in black.'

Gabriel. The drizzle had started. I wondered if it always rained at funerals. It had been overcast and now it was drizzling, tears falling from heaven to add to the tears of the bereaved.

My earpiece crackled again. 'We've photos.'

'Roger that.'

So, at the funeral, we had the man whom I thought did the deed. Perhaps, just perhaps, the killer-needing-closure theory was correct. I'd never been to the funeral of a person I'd killed or even visited their grave. Then again, I'd never tortured anybody. I decided I'd had enough gloom for one day and said into the radio, 'Let's get out of here.'

'Willco, out.'

I needed to get home to my personal misery, talk to my

new yellow friend Sam and being in the graveyard hadn't helped.

Things weren't going well. Death was all around us, or perhaps I was just becoming depressed. Kitty got a message that Susan Thomas had been killed. Some electrical generator thing called a Houchin being towed by a tractor had broken free and run into a group of people. She was the only one injured and she was dead. I felt terrible about that and I didn't even know the woman. I think my own personal circumstances were dragging me down.

Kitty was on the ball, though. She, by some magic, had got the post-mortem report and talked to somebody who was involved in the investigation. Apparently, there were absolutely no oddities about the death. It was an accident. Susan Thomas was just in the wrong place at the wrong time. She'd absolutely no illnesses and her organs were in nearly perfect order. Oops, what was the 'nearly' then? She was apparently a very normal, healthy young woman who couldn't have children. It seemed she'd had an abortion that had gone wrong. Kitty had Gaygan dig a bit. The abortion occurred when Susan was at university, so not connected to this case but what did come up, as Gaygan put it, 'quite by accident', was that Susan Thomas had absolutely no body hair: not one single hair from her feet to the hairline on her head. Not only that, she regularly attended a beauty salon for a treatment. She'd been subjected to controlled pulses of filtered light to remove unwanted hair, apparently damaging the follicle along with its ability to regenerate. Normally, this is only applied to unwanted hair but she'd done the lot apart from her head. She'd also undergone scarification and laser treatment of her skin. I thought it was extreme but apparently porn stars do it as well as lots of normal women. Well, perhaps porn stars are normal (I know what I mean).

Gaygan dug a bit further and came up with the fact that

Susan was hopelessly in love with a certain Sergeant Phillips. A scroll through her papers and computer had shown an extraordinary devotion to the man. That made two women devoted to Jase: Susan Thomas and Celia Foley. Well, more than two but two dead ones – both hairless, as were the murder victims, so the question was, was the hairlessness part of the relationship with Jase, or was it part of the murder sequence or was it some bizarre coincidence? But we knew the hairless thing had started when Jase was at school. The more information we got the less it made sense. On the other hand, the logical solution remained intact. I sometimes felt the whole world was mad and that definitely included me.

36

We invited Gabriel Holt in for questioning and he came complete with his brief, Mr Nathan Carstairs. As I observed Nathan Carstairs enter the interview room my impression was that I'd be surprised if he'd handled a case that could be a murder case or anything serious. I couldn't imagine a serious criminal wanting him as his brief and he wasn't on the local duty solicitor register. Protecting people accused of indecent exposure and, at a stretch, importuning I could see he may have some expertise and may be practised, but maybe I misjudge him due to the clothes, mince and lisp. I had this stray and totally inappropriate idea that he would be more appropriate selling a service other than a legal one to a defined minority market.

I watched Kitty and Gaygan. We had some identification of women from Wright, now we needed to get identification from Holt and explore why he was at the funeral. We'd sent pictures and information on both Wright and Holt to Heartlybridge and Exeter but nothing was back yet. In fact, Chief Inspector Snowden had not progressed one inch. Not that I was surprised. I just couldn't work out how he had made a senior rank.

Gabriel was once again immaculate; he should have been a fashion model. He had the slim, lithe and shaped build of the people that you see in clothes magazines. I doubt he was short of partners. He was again in a black shirt with pearl buttons and immaculately pressed trousers. Now his

181

makeup was faultless. The only difference was that he was wearing designer glasses: slim, square with black tinted lenses and I think they may be by Diesel but only because Gaygan had mentioned the make. That was another mystery to me. How would anybody be able to recognise the designer label of a pair of glasses? I only saw his eyes when he removed the glasses to read. The tired lines round them were either well covered or weren't there. He was also wearing a fawn, tailor-made, cashmere and silk, single-breasted jacket, with a very dark tartan lining. It must have cost a fortune. Either Gabriel had come into money or he was being paid a lot for his services, whatever they were. He was playing poofta again. He held his hands before him, limp-wristed, and moved them, keeping time with his speech. He held his right hand up, palm forward with a gentle flick if he wanted to stop the conversation. Was this act for us or was he hiding from us? Kitty and I knew a fine man who had served his country in the infantry was sitting there.

The photo identification procedure was as before. We'd tarted it up a bit and added some images, particularly Debbie Carter and Louise Bennett, who had given us pictures to help with our enquiries, and we had pictures of the two missing women, Linda Mercer and Penny Allan. Gabriel worked through them. He recognised Ghadah Qasim from Iraq and Rababa, who worked in the law office in Baghdad. Claire Forest and Andonella were also clearly recognised but he didn't know their names. He'd gone to a gymkhana with Michael, and Jase had been there with them. He thought he'd seen Vikki Coombes but didn't know where. He knew Celia Foley and Josephine Billinghurst were policewomen. He also knew Otis Brockett and Hashi Syedain, though he went very quiet when we asked him about them. It was as before but all four new photos were identified. He knew Debbie Carter and Louise Bennett had been with Jase and he'd seen Linda Mercer and Penny Allan. He confirmed that Penny Allan had been in a pub with Wright. I was still amazed that some women with responsible jobs would even contemplate being seen with someone like Wright. It made no sense to me but why should it? I'm not a responsible woman.

Using the pictures had advanced us a little in terms of confirmations but not much further. It was time to explore new ground. Kitty put me in the hot seat.

'Gabriel, I'd like to explore Jase a bit. Is that all right?'

Gabriel looked relieved and nodded.

'Did Jase have any other girlfriends that you know?'

'Yes, quite a few.'

'Have you any names?'

He looked at his brief who nodded. 'Yes, let me see...' He paused. 'Pauline Quick. She was a private in Iraq and she had a mate, Corporal June Johnston, a Scottish girl from Glasgow. I don't know if Jase went out with June Johnston but Wrighty did, I think.'

'Do you know what happened to them?'

'Happened to them?'

'Where they are now?'

'No, as you move about you lose touch, not that I really knew them.'

Here were two more we needed to locate.

'Others that went out with Jase?'

'Well, there was Lesley Marshal, Michelle Goldman, a woman named Peach and another was Carol Berger and my sister.'

'Your sister?'

'Christ, you don't have to sound so bloody surprised.' I was only surprised that Gabriel knew.

'I'm sorry.'

'Jase went out with her a couple of times when we were on leave. She thought he was wonderful. She was really pissed off when he didn't reply to her letters after we went back to Iraq.'

'Could we speak to her about him?'

'I don't see why not.'

'Can we have an address and phone number?'

'Sure it's 45 Cuthbert House, Wentover Street, Annetfield.'

'Do you know the postcode?'

'No, but it's near Newcastle and before you ask, I don't have a phone number. She rings me regularly and I keep meaning to ask but then I forget. She's lived there for about a month.'

'Oh, what's her name?'

'Patsy, well, Patricia.'

'Her surname?'

'Oh, yes, O'Donnell, though that's not the name of the guy she's living with.'

'The woman Peach you mentioned; was that a first name or her surname?'

'I reckon it was just a nickname.'

'That's great, Gabriel. Thank you for that.'

'Any others?'

'Women you mean? Yes. Look, Jase was like a pop star. They were all over him. Some of the other guys were really pissed off by it.'

'What guys?'

'Well, Wrighty for a start. He went wherever Jase went just to pick up the cast offs. Not sure it did him much good, though.'

'So, he didn't get much talent?'

'No, he's a crude bastard.'

'When did you last see him?'

'Dunno.' Gabriel had withdrawn. He was openly chatting about Jase and one specific question about Wright and you could feel the distance.

'Do you like him?'

'He's okay I s'pose.'

'So you do like him?'

He shrugged. More like a dismissive twitch. No, Gabriel didn't like Malcolm Wright.

'Did Michael like him?'

'Dunno.'

'Come on, Gabriel. You were closer to Michael than his mother. You knew who he liked and didn't like.'

'He liked Jase a lot, but he didn't like Wrighty.'

'Why not? He employed him.'

'I don't know. He just didn't.'

'Ah well, we can't like everyone.'

37

'The last time we questioned you we asked about some murdered women and you assured us that Michael couldn't have killed them.' It was then I fell in. How stupid I'd been. No wonder I was uncomfortable. I knew I'd missed something and I had no idea what. We'd just made the assumption that Gabriel knew about the murders, but we didn't think to question this. He never once queried the facts of the killings. I'd missed it, Kitty had missed it and Gaygan had missed it.

'How did you find out about the murders, Gabriel?'

'You told me.'

'I don't think so. You already knew.'

Gabriel looked at his hand on his lap. His head was down and shoulders slumped. He mumbled, 'You're just trying to trick me.'

'Come on, Gabriel. How did you know about the murders? We can play you the tapes if you want. You've your own copy.' I could see and feel Kitty next to me. She now recognised what I had recognised.

Nathan Carstairs said, 'Ma'am, gentlemen, I'd like a break to talk to my client.'

'Okay,' said Kitty. 'I'll have some tea and biscuits sent in. How long a break would you like?' Now she was being very considerate.

'A quarter of an hour should be sufficient.' There was a different Carstairs sitting opposite us. He spoke firmly, no effeminate lisp, his shoulders were back and firm, he was like a different man with the emphasis on man. Will I never understand sub-cultures?

We went into the canteen and got tea while a constable took tea and biscuits to the interview room.

'Christ, that was a cock-up,' said Kitty.

'Not really. I just fell in and we now have a suspect or witness who has to explain himself. He can explain the serial killings without admitting to how he found out and in doing so may give us some leverage on Celia's killing.'

Refreshed, re-planned and replenished, we returned to the interview room, but Carstairs asked us for another quarter of an hour. Kitty agreed. Another tea, more biscuits, a pee and it was time to try again.

Carstairs opened. 'My client wishes to make a statement.'

Kitty responded, 'Thank you. Would you like to go ahead, Gabriel?'

'I served in the Royal Southumbrian Fusiliers with Major Michael Carmichael. He was a brave and noble soldier. In the course of our service we became close and had a personal relationship. In the course of that relationship it became clear that Major Carmichael was engaged in an illicit enterprise of smuggling drugs. The enterprise was managed and run by Sergeant Jason Phillips.' It was clear that the solicitor had written this statement. 'Sergeant Phillips had a number of accomplices including Flight Lieutenant Susan Thomas of the RAF and Private Malcolm Wright.

'Sergeant Phillips maintained control by the use of blackmail. He was blackmailing Major Carmichael and me over our relationship and he knew of the rape of a number of women by Private Wright. I don't know what hold he had over Flight Lieutenant Thomas. Although he had the blackmail threat we were complicit in the business of drug smuggling and made a lot of money.

'In an attempt to break the hold of Sergeant Phillips on Private Wright, Private Wright murdered some women who'd had a relationship with Sergeant Phillips. Private Wright told Major Carmichael and they had a plan to expose Sergeant Phillips as the murderer.

'Sergeant Phillips discovered what had happened and in collusion with Corporal Munro found a way to kill Major Carmichael.' Tears were running down Gabriel's face and he wiped them away, messing up his makeup. We had another break to allow him to settle then Kitty restarted the questioning.

'Thank you, Gabriel. We now have a clearer picture of the series of murders of women. You knew that Wright had killed some women. When did you find out how they were murdered?'

'You're not going to leave me alone, are you?'

I had no idea what prompted the question. It was puzzling.

'Gabriel, we need to know about Celia,' I said.

Tears flooded down his face again. He was in no state to answer any questions but we needed to pin the murders down to gain a conviction.

'Not until we killed her.' His answer made no sense. It didn't relate to anything we'd asked.

'We? Who are "we"?'

'Wrighty and me.'

'So why did you and Malcolm Wright kill Celia Foley?'

'We thought she knew. We thought that Jase had told Sergeant Billinghurst to try to get out of prison. He got killed in prison so we thought the people who got him banged up needed to keep him quiet. It all went quiet so we reckoned we were okay. Then she got shot, you know, Sergeant Billinghurst, and you got shot, but we weren't picked up so you didn't know, so we had to make sure she didn't know.' He was verging on incoherence. 'It was horrible.

188

Wrighty raped her and beat her with a cane but she said she didn't know anything. He said that's what he'd done to the others. Then he burned her with a candle and with cigarettes. Well, we couldn't let her go so he strangled her.'

'And you just stood by and let him?'

'Yes.'

'Didn't she scream when you burnt her?' asked Kitty

'She couldn't.'

We stayed silent. Gabriel just looked at the floor. He was crying again. We waited.

Carstairs gave him a handkerchief and said, 'Gabriel.'

Gabriel looked up. 'We used one of those gag things that they have in S&M places.'

'S&M?'

'You know, sadomasochism.' We stayed silent. 'You know, it's like a rubber ball on a rope and it jams their mouth open.'

I took over as Kitty was trembling beside me. 'So, let me get this right – Gabriel, look at me. Look into my eyes.'

He looked at me. He was trembling.

'You tied Celia to a chair with her hands tied to the back of it so she was sitting across where you'd removed the seat and tied her legs to the back legs of the chair. You gagged her with this ball on a rope and then you burnt her sexual organs with a candle.'

He was staring at me. Tears streamed down his face. He was sobbing and trembling. He moaned and coughed as if he was going to be sick. The full horror of what he'd done impacted him. He started jerking. It was as if I was hitting him with a hammer. His nose started to run and his mouth hung open. I was concerned. I'd seen injured men in a bad way but this was much worse.

'We need a break for my client to gather himself,' Carstairs said in a concerned, timorous voice. He was also in a bad way.

189

'Gaygan, get the FME. Tell him we have an acute stress reaction.'

The doctor took about ten minutes to get to Gabriel. She came equipped with an injection and took him into another room. When she came back she said, 'I don't know what you did to him but he was hiding something and you brought it to the surface. He should be okay. He has rationalised what he has done but no more questions today.'

'Will he be okay tomorrow?'

'Probably. I will see him tomorrow morning but somebody should be with him until then just in case.'

Carstairs immediately volunteered, so we fixed bail, a time to return and the pair of them left.

38

'How are you two doing?' I asked Kitty and Gaygan.

'In need of a drink,' said Kitty. 'Let us repair to the local hostelry, as it says in the book I'm reading.'

'Sounds like Dickens.'

'Same time, but not him.'

'Must be George Eliot.'

'The problem with public schoolboys is that the bastards have been educated. That will cost you a drink.'

'We left for the Blue Bells.'

The Blue Bells was a wonderful little two-room pub tucked away in a back street. It wasn't my choice but was an old favourite of the local nick. It was a free house with a good selection of beers. Not that that mattered to us, we were all spirits people. The pub was almost empty, but it was still only 6 p.m. Gaygan mentioned he was hungry in that quiet polite way he has and I suppose that was the trigger.

The food was definitely of the bar food variety, so we weren't expecting an amazing meal.

A friendly guy who appeared to be the bartender seated us right away. He let us know that our server, Lisa, would be right over.

Lisa was something to behold. She must have been six feet, six inches tall. Slim with a bust that could compete in the all England championship, and she carried them well.

DC Debora Mackenzie, an efficient officer on Kitty's

team, wandered in and joined us. She was looking miserable. I don't think I had ever seen her miserable before.

'Problems?' I asked.

'Yes, s'pose.' She was on the brink of tears.

'Want to tell us?' asked Kitty.

'S'pose.'

'Go on then.' said Kitty.

'Well I had this boyfriend and I was a bit overweight and he chucked me.'

'Because you were overweight?'

'Yes, s'pose.'

'So I went to the gym, dieted and lost weight, I am now just on eleven stone. I started dating Roger, the trainer at the gym. He's smashing, you know, fun and incredibly fit.' She had a slight blush.

'Go on.'

'Well, I was invited to meet his mum and dad tonight. You know, dinner and all. So I went round. I went in and his mum said, "Have a seat". So I sat down on the settee. It had big round cushions.' She went silent. I thought she was going to cry. I think we were all puzzled.

'And?' I said.

'I sat on the cat and killed it.'

The silence lasted for about five seconds then we all burst out laughing.'

Debbie looked at us and she started to laugh.

I suppose that set the tone for the evening.

Lisa seemed to find Gaygan of particular attraction, which apparently was unusual and embarrassing for him.

The nice man who seated us came over and asked if he could get some drinks. I ordered a G and T, the females of the group followed suit and Gaygan opted for some fruit juice. Kitty winked at the barman and I suppose it was a vodka or gin that went into Gaygan's glass.

Lisa brought our drinks, and stood behind Gaygan and at

opportune moments bent or leaned forward so her bust rested gently against him much to his embarrassment and our covert amusement.

As for the food, Kitty had the Ted Smith (a roast beef sandwich with cheese and two fried eggs on top), I had the steak frites, Debora had scrambled eggs and Gaygan had another fruit drink that he hadn't ordered, some fruity thing that was the preserve of vegetarians, that perhaps was laced with alcohol, and he giggled when Lisa accidently on purpose molested him with her bust. The conversation was light and jokey, typical Met humour and much of it aimed at distracting Gaygan as additional alcohol went covertly into his glass.

Lisa cleared our plates and brought the bill, which Kitty and I split. The problem was what were we going to do with Gaygan as he was by now under the weather and grinning a lot. Lisa joined the discussion and it was decided she would look after him, to which he now readily agreed, so Debora phoned for a taxi and Lisa took Gaygan away, to where we had no idea.

The next day at 10.00 a.m. we were reassembled and ready to go. Gabriel seemed okay if a little quiet.

Kitty spoke to Carstairs. 'Before we start, I think you may like to look again at your client's statement.'

Carstairs looked puzzled.

'In the statement, Holt said, "Private Wright murdered some women who'd had a relationship with Sergeant Phillips". I think you need to confirm the truth of that statement. Thank you. We'll take a ten-minute break. I'll have tea sent in.' She did the bit about us leaving the room for the tape then Carstairs put his arms around Gabriel and it looked as if were both about to cry. The shock from the previous day was still evident.

We returned after ten minutes but they had not recovered. The tea sat on the table getting cold so we left for another ten minutes. We returned and Carstairs and Gabriel had, to some extent, recovered. The room was silent. We reintroduced the questioning.

'Do you stand by your statement, Gabriel?'

'I made a mistake. Wright murdered women who were senior to or managed the women Jason Phillips had a relationship with.'

I felt the hand of Carstairs again in the statement.

'How do you know that, Gabriel?'

'I just do.'

'How?'

'He would brag about it.'

'You didn't report it?'

'No, I was scared.'

'But he didn't kill you, Gabriel. Why didn't he kill you?' Kitty asked.

'He couldn't.'

'Why not?'

'I'd written down about the drugs and the murders and the blackmail and everything and I'd given it to Nathan to give to the police should I be killed.'

I looked at Carstairs and he avoided eye contact.

'That was clever, Gabriel. Where did you get that idea from?' asked Kitty.

'Don't answer that or you may just get Nathan into deep shit, so to speak,' I said. 'Kitty is going to charge you with a whole raft of things, including accessory to murder. You'll probably go to prison but because of your help and if you plead guilty, it won't be for very long. All we have to do now is pin down Malcolm Wright. Do you understand, Gabriel?'

'Yes, sir. I'm sorry, sir. I know if I'd come forward when Jase was charged then it would have been different but, yer know.'

I had a feeling that if he'd come forward at an early stage he might just have collected a hit man's bullet and none of this would be known. But I still wasn't convinced we had the story. Bits seemed to be missing, but I was sure we had enough.

'One last question, Gabriel; why did Corporal Munro help Sergeant Phillips?'

'Easy. Everybody loved Jase. He was a hero, had a CGC. He was always by your side in a fight. He was always there to get you out of trouble. He was always there when you wanted something.'

'Was it just you and Munro who loved him?'

'Christ, no. The entire platoon did. They agreed what they'd tell you at the investigation. Well, it was all true except Jase didn't have to fire. We all knew the major was out of it.'

'But you, Malcolm Wright and Major Carmichael were going to set him up for murder.'

Gabriel looked at his hands. They were clasped, fingers interlocked. 'I didn't want to do that. It was Wrighty's idea and Michael talked to somebody, I think his dad, and was told not to do it. Anyway, we didn't do it.'

'Tell me about Jase. Anything else? Anything odd?'

'Not really.'

'You said the entire platoon loved him. They covered for him. Yet you said, "Sergeant Phillips maintained control by the use of blackmail. He was blackmailing Major Carmichael and me over our relationship and he knew of the rape of a number of women by Private Wright. I don't know what hold he had over Flight Lieutenant Thomas. Although he had the blackmail threat we were complicit in the business of drug smuggling and made a lot of money." Was that true Gabriel?'

'Not really. He knew all those things but we wanted to work with him. It was Wrighty really.'

'What was "Wrighty really"?'

'We knew what he had done, killing the women and all. He's crackers.'

'Why did you go with him to kill Corporal Foley?'

'That was because Wrighty said that she would say that she would tell you lot that Michael did the murders and he would kill her but it wasn't like that. He tortured her to find out what she knew and she didn't know anything and we had to kill her then.'

'"We had to kill her", Gabriel.'

'Well, Wrighty strangled her.'

Gabriel was emotionally drained and clearly exhausted, so Kitty closed the interview and set bail. We agreed he would come back to sign a statement. What was clear was that Gabriel had the gist of the story but not the full facts, which is often the situation. I was bushed, so I went home, but Kitty wanted to do the report.

39

As soon as I got in, my internal phone started to ring.

'Sir, there's a member of the Salvation Army here to see you,' I was told.

'Okay, Charles. Give her ten pounds and I'll give it to you tomorrow or leave it with George.'

'No, sir, she wants to see you.'

'Why? No, what's her name?'

'Vera Theaston.'

I had no idea who she might be and then I fell in – Vera, Salvation Army. 'Please send her up, Charles.'

I did a quick removal of detritus and papers and waited about ten seconds before the doorbell rang. I opened it to be confronted by Vera, resplendent in uniform, white short-sleeved blouse with a closed collar and a navy skirt. She had a bag with the strap over her shoulder and a bowler-type hat on.

'Come in, Vera.' I led her way down the passageway into my lounge. 'Have a seat.'

'Can we sit at the table, Jake?'

'Sure.'

She moved to my dining table and sat on the opposite side to me.

'What can I do for you, Vera?'

'I wanted to check that you were okay.'

'Shouldn't I be?'

'You've been through a stressful time recently and lost Samantha and I may be able to help.'

'Vera, thank you. Would you like a cup of tea, coffee?'

'Sit there, Jake.'

She got up, took two glasses from a kitchen cabinet – she knew where they were – opened the freezer, put some ice in the glasses and then topped them up with water from the tap.

'How did you know where things are?' I asked.

'It must be my supernatural powers.' She laughed. 'No, before you first joined us you were working for MI5. A woman named Frances came to see Sir Nicolas. If I remember correctly there was some problem about the authenticity of some evidence. She came and talked about you and she'd also investigated a sergeant, let me see, Sergeant Billinghurst. Later, I had to come here to check some information, so I know where things were and I just assumed you'd leave them there.'

'You think I need help, Vera?'

'You, I think, are one of those people who can cope with any trauma.'

'Thank you, Vera. I do get lost and I'm in pain but I'll fight it and ignore it and I won't dwell on it and I'll live in hope that one day there'll be no pain, but all the time there is I'll deliberately do things I would have done before the reason for the pain came into my life. Is that clear or is it muddled?'

'I believe for you, Jake, it's clear. It seems you're taking Samantha out of your life. It may free you until you're fully in balance but at some stage you'll have to let her back in.'

'Vera, Sam will always be in my life but she's now lost and I must assume that's forever.'

'Wash out the past, Jake. Start again. No thinking of what might have been, no thinking about taking action. Start again.'

My phone rang and I answered. It was Kitty.

'Your young West Country lady has turned up trumps.'

'Can you hang on a minute please, Kitty. I've a guest and she's just leaving.'

'She?'

'Yes, Vera.'

'The Wicked Witch of the West?'

'Yes.'

'I'd best be quiet or she'll cast a spell on me.'

I pressed the silence button and put the phone down.

I turned and Vera was at the door. 'Be careful of that one, Jake, but if you need to talk I'm a good listener.' She slipped through the front door. 'Jake, please don't rush into filling the empty space,' she told me, and pulled the door closed behind her. I knew she meant Kitty.

No sooner had Vera gone than my doorbell went. It was George. I waved him in and switched on the phone.

'Okay, Kitty, go on.'

'See, you even know who I mean.'

'Kitty, please.'

'I'll pick you up at seven.'

'Are we going to the West Country?'

'No. Hereford.'

'This evening?'

'Yes, an early start there tomorrow.'

40

George was hovering in the hallway.

'Excuse me, sir, I want to say how sorry I am that your young lady has left and Miss Phillips, who is staying on the second floor, who was friendly with Miss Samantha, would like to talk to you.'

I didn't know Miss Phillips and at that moment didn't want to, nor did I know Sam knew any other people in the apartments and I only had a nodding acquaintance with them. 'Okay George.'

'She's downstairs, sir, and has some tickets to the National Gallery where there's an Impressionist exhibition.'

'Okay, George. What's her name?'

'Cynthia, I think, sir.'

I went down in the lift and an attractive young woman was by the desk. George introduced us.

'Oh, Captain Robinson, I so wanted to meet you. It seems to me that you're a mystery man and disappeared for such a long time, and well, Samantha didn't talk about you much, but clearly she...' She carried on talking while I absorbed the sight of her. She was a young woman, American; probably no older than mid-twenties with long blonde hair that just tumbled down over her shoulders. She was wearing a white dress with a V-neck and an elasticated waist, and it was very short, showing her long, slim, well-formed suntanned legs. She was only lightly made-up, perhaps only lipstick, but she didn't need makeup and, as far as I could tell, she'd only two pieces of jewellery, a fine chain around her neck with a stick of gold on the end of it and a small watch with a slim gold strap on her wrist. Despite the simplicity she was able to wear these modest clothes and look attractive in them.

'Whoa!' I raised my hands to stop her. 'Sam's gone and it seems we'll both miss her and you're the second person today that has a mission to console me in some way, but it'll take some time for me to recover. Second thing, I'd love to go to the art gallery with you but I know absolutely nothing about art.' I knew I'd seen her before but I didn't know where and I was sure it wasn't here in the building. 'Shall we go on the tube?'

We chatted on the underground and it seemed she came from Washington and a friend was renting the apartment so that she could see London. She, therefore, had a wealthy friend. Her questions weren't intrusive and I answered them so we were getting on well. She asked about me meeting Sam and the jobs we were doing at the chambers. She knew all about Sam's job and found mine as the personal detective for Sir Nicolas fascinating. She was very skilful at extracting information, so in the main I talked unless it impacted on reality and I was pleased I'd been fully briefed on cover stories. I wish I'd been as good as she was at her age. My problem was how I was going to find out what she really wanted. Was she a journalist? Was I being set up for something?

We got off at Charing Cross and passed into the hall in which the Impressionist exhibition was being held. A lecturer was standing before a large painting explaining to a group of seven students, five of whom were hanging on his every word with two at the back more interested in each other than the picture, one, a superior, well-dressed, young man who was being intently admired by a young woman whose eyes were large and soft in admiration with a prominent yellow pimple on her chin. The lecturer was saying, ' . . . Monet did share with Manet, however, a concern for representing actual scenes of the modern life of that time, rather than contrived historical, romantic or fanciful subjects such as Delacroix's 'La Liberté guidant le peuple'. Thus, for example, Monet's 'Déjeuner' was an extension, by virtue of a more immediate empiricism, of the realism of Courbet.'

When I hear this sort of shit I wonder what the hell they're talking about.

'Here' – he pointed towards the picture with an elegant, languid gesture that matched his laid back, aloof presentation – 'as you can see, the subject matter involves a domestic scene featuring his wife, son and garden. This was common in this period of...'

An assemblage of chattering schoolchildren, more interested in talking to each other than seeing the exhibits in the gallery, passed between the group of students and us, their teacher attempting to keep them together as a cohesive group. The disruption subsided as the children moved on and once again the lecturer's affectation broke through.

'...to fragment his brushstrokes into the characteristic broken touches that are the hallmark of impressionist style.'

'Well, what do you think of art then, Jake?' asked Cynthia.

This was an invitation to be negative, which I attempted to suppress, as I rather liked the picture that was the centre of the rapt attention of five of the seven students and four other visitors. 'Art, like that picture, I like and would welcome on my wall, apart from not having space on my wall and its artificial price as it lacks intrinsic value.'

I must have spoken more loudly than I intended because the lecturer stopped mid-flow and the group's eyes swivelled towards this philistine that would utter such a materialistic condemnation.

'What the fuck does that mean?' said one of the students.

The structure and vocabulary of his question indicated he disagreed quite venomously.

'Um, let me use a pork chop and a gun as examples. You remember the Haiti earthquake? Perhaps you don't, but many people were left homeless and starving. Well a pork chop would have more value than that picture because you can eat it and the gun would have even more value as you could shoot a whole pig and guard your kill against others stealing it. That picture, by comparison, only has an artificial value resting on what somebody is prepared to pay for it but there's no *intrinsic* value in that.' All were staring at me now and the eyes were hostile.

'Surely, the sheer beauty and uniqueness gives it value.' This was the smartly dressed young man, his attention distracted from the girl with the pimple.

'As I think some ancient Greek said, beauty is in the eye of the beholder, and as for uniqueness, a canvas I might paint would have that quality. No, the value lies in a belief engendered by the art world that pictures or other objects have this mysterious quality called art that's only understood by a few educated into an art culture and some of that art has a greater monetary value than other pieces so designated.' I was using the contorted English that the lecturer had used to express his superiority.

There was a silence being driven into some students by the sheer effrontery I was displaying, anger in others and a range of emotion in the rest.

'Really!' exclaimed the trembling lecturer, totally overcome by indignation that somebody could possibly express such a view.

'I think we'd better go,' said Cynthia with some feeling.

I smiled as we walked towards the door, sensing the hostility in the eyes that followed us. Cynthia stopped, looked at me and said, 'You don't really believe what you said do you?'

'I've no idea. I think that Monet picture is great and I'd love to look at it every day but would it give me more satisfaction than a picture I liked, bought for a couple of hundred pounds? I really don't know. What I do know is that if I was starving I'd go for a pork chop rather than a picture of any sort.'

'But when you've eaten the pork chop you'd have nothing but that picture will go on for your lifetime.'

'Sort of, but without the pork chop I die, so I don't need a picture if I'm dead.'

'You're just an uncultured wretch.' She smiled.

'Okay, I'll buy you a little picture at that art shop in the High Street or afternoon tea, your choice. I'll still have afternoon tea and while I do you can look at the picture if that's your choice.'

'But after you've had your tea I'll still have the picture.'

'True, very true. So it all depends on it being a life or death situation. What will it be then?'

'Tea.'

'Good, come on then, Derceto,' I said.

'What is that supposed to mean?'

'Derceto was a goddess, the wife of Dagon, the principal deity of the Philistines and clearly you think I'm a philistine.'

She smiled, the even-toothed smile that epitomises Americans. 'I suppose you see yourself as Dagon.'

'No, I'm El.'

'Who was he then?'

'When the Philistines took on the Canaanite religion, Dagon became number two to El.'

'How do you know all this shit?' Now that phraseology wasn't in keeping with the portrayed background so who was Cynthia and what was her role?

'Ah, I opted for a classical pre-history course when I was at school on the grounds that I'd be the only one in the class and so I'd be able to bunk off. Unfortunately, I had a teacher who was very keen on all this classical pre-history stuff and I got to enjoy it.'

'They'll bloody lock you up, Jake.'

'I remember Samantha telling me that and the English phraseology from an American is interesting.'

'Ah ha! I think both Samantha and I are right.'

After our afternoon tea with buttered crumpets we went back to the apartments and parted in the lift. She was definitely some sort of investigator, but for whom or what I'd no idea. I think she was testing something but what I could only wonder. The next day she was gone or so George told me.

41

I got changed, threw some clothes in a bag and my doorbell went. It was Kitty. Ten minutes later we were heading out of London.

'Please tell me what's going on.'

'Well, Alison was concerned that Celia Foley's body was found in Ipplden. It's such an odd place to find a body so whoever did the killing there must have known the area, so she did a hunt through the local authority for the names Holt, Wright and a couple of others we'd mentioned, including Foley. Well, there was a Wright in, of all places, Ipplden. So she went to visit and lo and behold she's our Malc's great aunt. And he came to visit her, he came by car and he had a mate with him, a very nice young man named Gabriel.'

'So how didn't the house-to-house find this?'

'Well, there's this police station full of very nice police-men and women who can't find grass on the village green.'

'I've the feeling that you're just spinning this out to annoy me.'

'Oh, it gets better. The old lady remembers the car.'

'Please, the suspense is killing me.'

'Well it was a large grey Volvo and it had an individual registration: GIL 10K.'

'Well, that's a start.'

'Oh, it gets much better. Your young lady had a chat with a sergeant in traffic in Exeter. They're friends and he did

206

some checks for her and came up with something interesting. The car in question belongs to Corporal Gil Hibberd. So I had a word with the RMP and they're holding
him and the car, and a forensic team are having a look at it
while we speak.'

'Where do we stay tonight?'

'Well, we can interview Hibberd first thing in the morning because the forensic boys won't finish till about seven
tonight and promised me a report by nine tomorrow
morning.'

'So why are we dashing over to Hereford tonight?'

'I decided that you needed some R and R before the
interview tomorrow.'

'Now that's very kind of you.' Danger bells were ringing
but what danger I had no idea, just a vague unease. I can be
so naïve sometimes

'Well, it wasn't entirely altruistic. I needed some stress-
relaxing excitement as well so I booked us into that nice
little hotel we visited the last time we were down there.'

'I see.'

'Well, I'm not sure you do.'

'I don't?'

'They only had one double room.'

I was saying nothing.

'So I booked it. So you'll have to share with me tonight.'

'I see. So I assume I'd better get some rest now then.'

'Yes, I suppose you'd better.'

So I did. I dozed in the car. Well, I tried to doze in the
car. I was troubled. Kitty and I had been tracked by car to
Bulford and it was almost as if they wanted to be seen. Then
Sam and I in our perambulations along the Chelsea
Embankment had been followed. It then dawned on me;
that was where I'd seen Cynthia. She'd been sitting on the
wall where we'd seen the cat. Sam had left to go to her
children and then the attractive young woman had made a

date and taken me to an art gallery. She was, or seemed to be, some form of investigator, or was she just bait to catch a predatory male and when that didn't work she just disappeared? Was all this to do with this investigation or was it something else? I was puzzled. The Family didn't need to track me; they knew what I was doing. Was the tracking of me to do with Sam going back to her husband and children? Perhaps I would never know.

42

At 9.00 a.m. the following day, having had breakfast with a very lively and energetic Kitty, and me in desperate need of R and R, we prepared for the interview. Did I have a conscience about Sam? No. I loved Sam. I suppose I always will but I have to move on. How the hell will I do that? Kitty wasn't the person I would move on with and she wouldn't want me to move on with her; she only had interest in me as a co-investigator and co-respondent in rest and relaxation Kitty-style.

I once asked one of my professors at university, a specialist in psychological anthropology, about the fact that after sex women were energetic and men were knackered. He said it was a biological imperative that enabled the woman to keep up with the faster, stronger man if the male of the species decided to run off. He did comment on my observation skills, but I thought he was pulling my leg. Now I'm not sure.

Gil Hibberd was brought into an interview room at Credenhill Barracks by an RMP sergeant and corporal.

'Good lord, Captain! I saw the name but I didn't know it was you,' said the sergeant.

'Good to see you, Mike. How's your charge?'

'All ready for you, sir, and here's the forensic report.'

'Thank you, Mike. Keep buddy boy here for a while and we'll see what the boffins can tell us.'

'I've a letter for the inspector.'

He handed it to Kitty and she read it and looked at me.

'It's straightforward. It's from a Colonel Metcalf who, it seems, is the commanding officer here. He wants us to accept his apologies for not meeting us and he says we've his full authority to pursue our investigations wherever they may lead. Now that's nice, isn't it? He says he'd be grateful if we keep him informed and he understands that the information will have to be kept confidential and anything we do tell him he'll treat as confidential. Let me see; he says if we find anything that may impact the operational efficiency of his unit he'd be grateful if we would inform him.'

'Okay, Sergeant, we'll read the boffin stuff and then we'll interview the corporal.'

The forensic report told us little. The car was immaculate but with some traces of the use of cocaine, a number of DNA samples of two people, but who we had no idea, and a multitude of Gil's prints. A second set and one set of Gabriel's prints were on the front wing. Gabriel must have leaned against it. All in all the limited evidence told us little apart from the fact that Gil had been up to some hanky-panky on the back seat with an unknown person and Gabriel had been near the car. No evidence that Celia had been in the car.

A solicitor turned up so we got started on the interview. Kitty did all the intro and formal stuff and I started to question.

'Gil, have you loaned your car or hired it out to anybody?'

'I'm not allowed to hire it.'

'Good, so you lent it out.'

'Might have.'

'Might have lent it to whom?'

'Friends.'

'Names please.'

'I don't remember.'

'Supposing I was to tell you that Malcolm Wright's fingerprints were found in your car. What would you say?'

'Bullshit!'

'Bullshit, I see. What about Gabriel Holt's fingerprints. What would you say?'

'No comment.'

'So, you lent Gabriel Holt your car and he went somewhere with Malcolm Wright. Why did you lend Gabriel your car?'

'Cos he wanted to go someplace.'

'Did you go with him?'

'No.'

'What place was it he wanted to go?'

'I dunno.'

'Did he tell you?'

'Yeah, but I don't remember.'

'Was it Exeter or Heartlybridge?'

'No, it was a funny name.'

'A funny name like Ipplden?'

'Yes, that's it. Ipplden.'

'So when was this?'

'Oh, it's gotta be three weeks now.'

'Did he look after your car?'

'Yes, it was all clean and polished inside and out. You didn't find any prints did you?'

'We found blood in your boot and at this moment it's being checked with the blood of Celia Foley, who was found murdered in Ipplden.'

'Christ, Captain, it wasn't me! I don't even know where Ipp-whatever is.'

'Now tell us what you do know.' It is amazing what an appropriate and convincing lie can reveal.

'Gabriel borrowed my car. He was upset. He said he had to go to this Ippl-place. So I lent it to him.'

'He was upset?'

'Yes, sort of scared.'

'Did he mention anybody else going with him?'

'No! Honest!'

'He didn't mention a woman that he and Wright may meet?'

'No, sir. I just lent him my car and he brought it back.'

'Did he mention Wright at all?'

'No, sir.'

'Did he say why he wanted a car? After all, he used public transport to come and get it and leave after he returned it.'

'No, sir. He just returned the car, clean and polished.'

'What was he like? Was he okay?'

'He seemed okay. Perhaps a bit quiet, but I just thought he was tired. I dropped him at the station.'

'Thank you, Gil. It'll be helpful if you can remember the dates.'

'It was a Tuesday. Last Tuesday of the month, last month that is.'

Kitty pressed some buttons on her mobile phone. 'So that would have been the twenty-seventh,' she said. 'That is only eight days.'

'I suppose. I couldn't be there 'cos I was here. I can prove it.'

'We're sure you can, Gil. You've been a great help. We'll write this up and get you to sign it and you'll be free to go. You may be called upon to be a witness if this goes to trial.'

With that, Kitty closed the whole thing off and I went into the lounge for a well-earned kip. Jase must have been bloody fit to have so many women on the go. I was struggling with one.

43

The next morning, we went to arrest Malcolm Wright. I hated these early morning arrests. It was 5.00 a.m. when we banged on the door of his first-floor flat, but there was no response. Clearly he wasn't home. The front door of the building was unlocked and there was evidence that somebody had been sleeping in the passageway. Well, there was nothing for it but to knock the door down, so we did.

The flat was a study in filth and it stank. It was one large room with two sash windows that looked out on to the street. A constable was attempting to open one and Gaygan the other. Eventually, the constable got his window open with a bang and it immediately crashed down again, so he propped it open with a piece of broken curtain rail. Gaygan surrendered with his one. At least some unpolluted air was circulating. How could anybody live in a place like that?

At one end of the room was the kitchen. There was an old-fashioned sink that must have come out of the ark. It had once been white and looked like glazed concrete from the numerous chips, but what was really striking was the sheer quantity of dirty crockery in it. There was green and grey mould and mildew growing on the surfaces of the crockery and it was from this heap that the smell was emanating. To the left side of the sink was a wooden draining board and it too was piled high with dirty dishes. How they didn't slip and crash to the floor could only be explained by the items being stuck together by the fungus and mould. It was revolting and made worse by the assorted debris strewn around it: packets, takeaway food containers, empty tins; it was like a badly kept refuse tip. It could have been a modern artwork by Tracey Emin, although there was no sexual connotation – well, there may have been but I don't understand art; I either like something or I don't and I didn't like this sink.

The extraordinary thing was that there was an equally prehistoric gas stove to the right of the sink and it was immaculate. It was white and mottled blue with black, iron fittings, and it gleamed. One could imagine it in a show-room of kitchen fittings sixty years ago and housewives of the time drooling over it.

The other end of the room had a pile of blankets heaped on a bare mattress on the floor. There was a cupboard and two chests of drawers. Two constables were tentatively opening and closing the drawers. They were wearing latex gloves and from the looks on their faces they wished they had masks over their noses and mouths, and goggles.

The real surprise was the wooden dining table in the middle of the room. Its top was covered with a gleaming sheet of glass, thick with ground edges. This was no spare windowpane. This was meant for a purpose and the purpose was related to drugs, as was the array of chemistry equip-ment in a cupboard between the windows. Again, this equipment was immaculately clean. How did he clean the equipment when the sink was a compost heap? Perhaps it had just been brought in. Then I noticed a flat, stainless steel sink in the bottom of a cupboard against the wall. A drain went through the wall and a tap fed by a copper pipe was above the sink. There were cardboard boxes stacked next to the cabinet. In the cardboard boxes were smaller containers of icing sugar and powdered milk and other similar substances that contained no names. There was also a cardboard box of small, clear, press-and-seal bags. Clearly, each was to contain a single hit of heroin or whatever street descriptor was in use.

As I looked around I began to assess the man who lived in this flat of contradictions. Clearly there was a multiple personality at work here. On the one hand we had a slob, on the other a meticulous, health-conscious person – well, health conscious from the point of view that he didn't want contaminated product. The third aspect was that he was a serial killer of women. All of this suddenly sparked a memory. We had been told that he was immaculately clean at school and his books were neat, but when he joined the army that all changed. We were also told he had high motivation to behave and be clean when at school; sex was used as motivation and reinforcement by his foster mother. Perhaps this was similar; drug business to reinforce the cleanliness and everything else didn't matter. Or in one area we had one personality and in another area we had a different personality. The problem was that we had no owner of the multiple personalities. Malcolm Wright had clearly done a bunk.

A policeman at a chest of drawers said, 'Ma'am,' and held up a ball with a rope through it. One more nail in the coffin of Malcolm Wright, so to speak.

A bedraggled young woman, resplendent in a threadbare dressing gown draped over her shoulders, wearing a very short, dirty, transparent nightdress that did nothing to enhance her modesty (or hide the fact that the carpet didn't match the curtains) wandered in from the hallway. She stood shivering by the side of Kitty then said, 'Malc ain't ere.' She was probably little more than a girl, but looked fifty and whined her statement over and over again. We got the message the first time and the repetition was like aggravating background music – no, more like the incessant, aggravating meow of my cat when she's hungry.

Kitty called over a young police officer, who was

desperately trying to look as if she was doing something but was actually doing nothing, and said, 'Annie, I'd like you to take Miss No-drawers here back to her room and find out everything she knows about Malcolm Wright. If the room is hygienic make a cup of coffee or something for her. On no account consume anything yourself. Look around and gain an impression to see if there's anything that may help us with our enquiry. Do you understand?'

'Yes, ma'am,' said Annie and left with the aptly named Miss No-drawers.

'She'll get nothing,' I said.

'You're correct, Jake, but it has some advantages. Firstly, it gets that useless excuse for a police officer out of my sight. Secondly, it'll stop half the police officers in this room peering at that girl's fanny – that includes you. Thirdly, Annie may catch something and be off sick for a while.'

I'd not thought of Kitty as at all vindictive but the last comment seemed as if she was.

'You don't seem very keen on PC Annie whoever.'

'She's probably great entertainment for the male officers in the locker room but as for police work she's a total waste of space.'

'Ah ha, I see.'

'I doubt if you do, Jake. It's still tough enough being a female in a male-dominated police service without the Annies of this world reinforcing mythical stereotypes and spending at least an hour a day shagging the chief inspector.'

I raised my eyebrows.

'Don't you look at me like that, Captain Goody Two-Shoes.'

'I'm sorry. I didn't know you wanted to shag the chief inspector. I thought you only had eyes for me.'

'Piss off!' she growled then she laughed.

44

Kitty had been on and off the phone from the time we got there. She'd pushed out an alert that she was seeking a serial killer, complete with description, and the police office had circulated a photo. Thank God for computers. Eventually, she got the call she had been waiting for; Wright was under arrest for an attack on one Gabriel Holt in a bar called the Eromeni. Holt, it seemed, was in the Royal Brompton. It was odd that he was at the Brompton as they specialised in heart and lung treatments. When we got there we immediately found out why. Gabriel was in a side ward with a police officer on the door. He was waiting for us. A doctor briefed us. Gabriel had been brought in last night. He'd been severely beaten by a man using a knuckleduster that had smashed his nose and left cheekbone and he had a fractured skull. He'd been stabbed and the blade had punctured his right lung. He was brought to the Brompton as the blade was still in his chest and there was concern that it might have damaged his heart. As it was, he was as well as could be expected but we could have no longer than ten minutes with him, and he wasn't to be disturbed either physically or emotionally. He was scheduled for further surgery, mainly cosmetic, that afternoon.

Gabriel was sat up at an angle in bed. He looked just as the doctor had described, with various dressings on his head and face. He was no longer a pretty boy. It was going to take a first-rate plastic surgeon to get him back to his former self.

'Hello, Gabriel. It looks like you've been in the wars.'

'You bastards. You told that arsehole Wright and he came after me. If I'd known I could have taken him but it was a total fucking surprise.'

Whoops! So much for 'don't disturb him'.

'Are you saying somebody told him you'd talked to us?'

'Oh, butter wouldn't fucking melt! Who else could have told him?'

We needed information here, not to defend ourselves. 'Gabriel, how do you know somebody told him that you talked to us?'

'How the fuck do you think. Just fucking look at me.'

'But it could be something else.'

'What else, smart arse? Anyway, he told me.'

'Told you what?'

'He said I was a grass and I shouldn't talk to the filth and he was fucking right.'

'Who told him, Gabriel?'

'Christ, it wasn't a fucking interview. Who else could it be but you bastards?'

'Gabriel, look at me. *Look at me.* Look into my eyes.'

He slowly turned his head towards me and looked into my eyes.

'Now, Gabriel, do you think I told him?'

He looked down and shook his head. 'No, Captain, but somebody did.'

'And I'm going to find out exactly who that somebody is, Gabriel. Now tell me anything that may give me a clue.'

He was now much calmer. 'I dunno. He just said I was a grass and then he let fly at me.'

'Was he on his own?'

'Course he was. He's always on his own.'

'What time were you attacked?'

''Bout seven.'

'So the latest Wright could have found out was about six-

218

thirty as he had to get to the bar, assuming he already had weapons. Did he come by car?'

'Dunno, but you can't park round the bar anyway.'

'He cleared his flat, so he knew he'd have to run, so he may have known about six.'

'When you're mended a bit I'll come back and see you, Gabriel, okay?'

'Captain.'

'Yes.'

'Sorry, I know you wouldn't tell, but I don't trust those rozzers.' He was looking at Kitty when he said it.

45

We walked down the stairs. How was I going to explore this?
As it turned out, I didn't have to as Kitty said, 'Jake, we've
got a leak and it's a dangerous leak.'

'So, tell me what you think.'

She stopped and caught my sleeve, turning me towards
her. 'You, Gaygan or I didn't do this. I did a summary report
and sent it to my boss.'

'That's Superintendent Urmee Khan.'

'Yes.'

'I remember, and he's at New Scotland Yard.'

'Right.'

'So you sent it by email?'

'Yes, at about five and that means he could have talked to
somebody before six and Gabriel was a dead duck so to
speak. What are we going to do, Jake?'

'Did you tell anybody else?'

'Of course: Rod Wilkes.'

'Give him a call; tell him what's happened. This may be a
Special Branch problem and he can talk with your boss and
inform him that he's the Special Branch link and nobody
else is.'

'I see. Let the politicians handle politics.'

'Kitty, I'm a simple copper with no promotion ambitions
and I'm seconded, so I'm of no consequence and invul-
nerable to coercion. You could get blocked or sidelined;

you need to get out from underneath so you're not shat on. Let Rod handle it.'

'You know it's a Special Branch problem don't you?'

'Well, in American football there are attackers, tacklers and blockers. The tackler is to stop the attacker running with the ball. The job the blocker has is to prevent the man running with the ball from being tackled. Well, we're running with the ball and we might score a touchdown and the key to our scoring is Gabriel, so if he doesn't give evidence a whole load of stuff doesn't come out about Golden Balls, including his endearing relationship with Gabriel. Remember the thought in The Family is that the haloed Michael is a serial killer and perhaps the message is that Gabriel has been picked up by the arch tackler, so I need to break confidence and block a particular superintendent by letting The Family know that Malcolm Wright is in the frame and Michael is in the clear.'

'You're talking about West aren't you?'

'Yes, so I'll just ring Rupert and Randolph.'

'You're talking about the Home Secretary and the Earl of wherever.'

'Yes, I think I might just be.'

'What will you tell them?'

'That Michael isn't the killer and that they have to stop West interfering if they're to get the result they want.'

'But what about the Gabriel–Michael relationship?'

'With a clear run at Wright, it disappears into the gloom and isn't seen.'

'And the drug running?'

'Well, with Wright pleading guilty to the serial killing and Gabriel properly briefed, the whole thing should just be a five-minute wonder full of gore on the front page focused on the murders, and disappear into history.'

'How do you know Wright will plead guilty?'

'Well there's this defence barrister named Sir Nicolas

221

Ross and a first-rate solicitor named Keith Todd and between them they might just convince him.'

'Christ, Jake, I'm glad you're on my side.'

46

Kitty's phone went. Wright had been sighted at Victoria Station and we set off with Gaygan driving, all blues and twos and rocking and rolling down the Kings Road, past Sloane Square onto Lower Grosvenor Gardens and round to Victoria Station. When we arrived there were six uniformed officers in the charge of an inspector named Argent, and they had no idea what Wright looked like. Kitty took over and had a uniformed officer placed at each exit with the inspector at the Underground. The three of us – Kitty, Gaygan and me – started at one end of the main concourse and headed towards the other end. Our phones were on, as I didn't have a radio. Luck plays an enormous part in any search and even more so in a crowded major train terminus.

I was walking down the platform side, Kitty in the centre and Gaygan along the shops, restaurants and arcades. It was slow. A large crowd was looking at the electronic timetable display that regularly clicked over showing arrival and departure times. My phone went. It was Kitty.

'Yes.'

'Arrival and departure display. Left-hand end, showing Gatwick, he is looking at it.'

I eased through the crowd and Kitty was with me, a couple of steps behind. I could hear her on her radio. Wright clocked me, turned to run and saw a copper. He spun round to face me, pushing a knuckle-duster onto his left hand and then had a knife in his right. A woman screamed and the crowd parted and he faced me backing towards the board.

'Okay Malc, not a good idea.'

'I'll kill you, you bastard.'

'No, definitely not a good idea Malc.'

A potty hero, with shit for brains decided to tackle Wright and the knife missed the idiot by an inch as I shouted at him to stand clear. Two constables were coming from the left with ASPs. And three others were moving back the members of the crowd that hadn't already retreated. With Gaygan by my side we closed on Wright. Gaygan had an ASP.

'Come on, Malc, let's go and have a talk.'

'Come on then, Captain, come and try on a real soldier.'

I pointed at the police and told them to stay.

'Okay Gaygan. When I have subdued him put on the handcuffs.' I don't know why I told him, he knew what to do. I started to stride towards Wright, he backed up to the barrier. Now he had to make a decision and he did, he charged to find the sole of my shoe in his stomach. He dropped the knife as he collapsed onto his knees. A ragged cheer went up from the observing crowd and probably fifty pictures were taken. Gaygan stood on Wright's left arm, removed the knuckle-duster, cuffed him and helped him to his feet.

47

It had already been a long day and it was only 7.00 a.m. We sat in the modern, well-equipped interview room in Belgravia Police Station on Buckingham Palace Road. But it didn't have the familiar ambience of Earls Court Road. I'd persuaded Keith to be the solicitor representing Wright and with some reluctance, he accepted my briefing. We were all systems go by 8.00 a.m. so Kitty cautioned Wright. And we would see him at 11.00 a.m. at the Earls Court factory. Inspector Argent and his sergeant took over to question him about the attack on Gabriel and promised to deliver him to us at Earls Court station at 11. We went for breakfast and then went back to Kitty's factory at Earls Court.

11.00 am came and Wright was delivered. He was not a happy bunny. Keith listened to what Kitty had to tell him and then sat with Wright in the interview room.

Kitty did the interview under caution spiel and then she, Gaygan, Wright and Keith ran through the identification bit for the tape recorder, and away they went. I watched the video of the questioning from the next room.

'Well, Malcolm, you do like to dig holes for yourself. Would you like to tell me about the death of, say, Claire Forest?' asked Kitty.

'Never heard of her.'

'Oh dear, Malcolm, you're not going to make hard work of this are you?'

'What's in it for me?'

'Not a lot,' said Kitty. 'You give us the information, we charge you with murder, you plead guilty and get a reduced sentence or not as the case may be. Or you protest your innocence, you get found guilty anyway and serve a longer sentence.'

'But you don't know nuffin,' insisted Wright.

'Why did you beat up your friend Gabriel?'

'He didn't know nuffin.'

'Then why did you beat him up?'

He sat and looked at her for ages and then he said, 'I knows you'll get me for that police bitch. She didn't know nuffin eiver and she wasn't even fun to kill.'

Just then the door to the observation room opened and an officer said, 'There's a call from the Brompton Hospital and it may be important.' It was Gabriel; his sister Patsy was there and she wanted to talk with me. I went back into the interview room and Kitty officially released me.

The Royal Bromptom was about a mile from the police station at Earls Court, so I walked. Patsy O'Donnell, Gabriel's sister, was waiting for me when I got to the hospital. She was her brother's female image, but not as tall. I must say they could have been sisters. She had the same hair, dyed black and it was shaped in the same way so that it swept back, covering her ears and stopped in a curve just level with her shoulders. Her eyebrows were black and her eyelashes were made up with mascara, and she favoured blue eye shadow just like her brother. She even gestured in a similar way, but she was more natural and feminine. Perhaps he'd mimicked his sister and now it was habitual.

She was nervous and smiled tentatively at me. We shook hands.

'Have you eaten?' As it was only 12.05 p.m. it was unlikely that she had.

'I've very little money.'

'Good, then I can take you to lunch.'

She smiled nervously. 'Gabriel said you were a nice man.'

'Ah, well, even he gets things wrong sometimes.'

She smiled properly.

'There's a Pizza Express just down the road. Would that suit you?'

She nodded.

'When did you last eat?'

'Well, um, yesterday morning.'

'And I bet that was cornflakes.'

She nodded again.

'Come on then. I don't want you fainting on me because you're starving hungry.'

We walked for five minutes then crossed the busy road and entered the Pizza Express. A member of staff took us to a table for two. Patsy was clearly out of her depth.

'Have you been to Pizza Express before?'

She shook her head.

'It's pretty good. Tell me the sort of things you like.'

'I don't know really.'

'You like spicy things, meaty things or cheesy things?'

'I suppose I like cheesy things.'

'Great, then we've come to the right place.'

The waiter brought menus. I ordered rustica tomatoes, garlic bread and a bottle of pinot grigio wine that we could have while we waited for the first course. We explored the menu and settled on bruschetta for both of us for starters, a quattro formaggi for Patsy and diavolo for me. I only ordered that because the menu said it was devilishly hot. She toyed with the tomatoes as we chatted about nothing: Gabriel joining the army, how she thought it odd he joined but how much he loved it, what it was like in the supermarket and how she hated it; she wanted to be a teacher but didn't have the qualifications to get started. Then the bruschetta arrived.

227

'Tell me about Jason Phillips.'

She stooped dead in her tracks. 'Why?' It almost snapped out.

'I want a picture of him that's different from mine.'

'What's your picture?'

'I liked Jase. I led the investigation into his killing of Major Carmichael and we got to know each other well, but I need a woman's view.'

She was hesitant. 'I went out with him you know.' She knew that I knew. She was just getting her head around how she would answer and then it came out in a rush. 'He was beautiful, just beautiful.' She paused, fighting to control her emotions. 'I fell in love with him the first time I saw him.' I waited. She was playing with her bruschetta. 'He had this way of making you feel you were the centre of the whole world. He'd ask you things and it was, sort of, as if he really wanted to know and he listened to what you said. Not like most men who have decided about something and just want you to agree with them. I just loved being with him. I felt protected. You're a bit like that. I feel safe with you but I was frightened of meeting you, you being an officer and all, but you aren't a bit stuck-up.'

'Thank you, fair lady.'

'Oh, I'm sorry. I didn't mean...' She was flustered.

'And I don't think you're stuck-up either.' She smiled.

'He was like that.'

'Like what?'

'He used to turn things on their head and laugh at himself and make you feel good about the silly thing you'd just done and he was not, not, I think the right word is condescending. He just accepted you as you were, warts and all.'

The waiter arrived with the pizzas and we ate in silence for a while. Patsy concentrated on her plate.

'Do you like it?'

'Yes, but there's a lot of it.'

'I know. I struggle a bit sometimes but my mum said I've to clean my plate. But now I'm happy to leave what I don't want.'

'See, you do it.'

'I do what?'

'You kinda make it okay.'

'And Jason did that?'

'Yes, he was wonderful. I still love him even though he's dead.' There were tears in her eyes and emotion in her voice. I let the silence sit until she recovered.

'You said Jason was beautiful.'

'Yes, it wasn't just the way he treated you; he was beautiful to look at. He had these broad shoulders and slim hips and super firm muscles – not all knotty like a body builder, but smooth and rippled and his skin was smooth and tanned, and your fingers just slipped over him, and he made love like a god.' She stopped. She'd become so lost in her description of Jase that she'd forgotten she was talking to me. Now she blushed and hunted in her handbag for her handkerchief, so I gave her mine. She then composed herself and ate some more pizza and I poured some more wine in her glass.

'Jason sometimes drank too much but he was never noisy or violent or anything. He just used to go quiet and then go to sleep.'

'How long did you go out with him?'

'Oh, on and off for about three years.'

I was staggered. I thought it was one leave period.

'That was a long time.'

'Not really. I knew him from school, though we didn't...you know. I only saw him when he was home on leave and he had other girlfriends.'

'How did you feel about that?'

'Okay I suppose. As long as he came to see me and let me love him it was okay.'

Here was a woman who knew the love of her life had other women and she just accepted it because she loved him so much. How strange.

'We had a son you know.'

This was a bolt from the blue. Gabriel thought they just had a short relationship and now I find out it was an extended relationship and they had a child.

'I didn't know. Where–?'

'He died, a cot death. That's what broke us up really.'

The silence went on for a while. She was deep in thought.

'You asked me about him being beautiful?'

I don't think I did but I let it run.

'He was perfectly smooth, no hair I mean. He was like little Jason – as smooth as a baby's bum he used to say. He used waxing on me so we both would be smooth. It was weird really but very sexy.' She stared directly into my eyes. 'I still am, you know. I don't have a hair on my body. My boyfriend loves it, but he's no Jason, all rush and panting and sweating. Jason used to take his time and he could do it over and over again and he'd send me right through the roof. Sometimes I had to scream.' She was staring directly into my eyes. She wasn't embarrassed. She was just saying it as it was for her. Now, what do you say, Jake?'

'Would you like some pudding?'

She laughed. No, she giggled, probably at the incongruity of my question, and said, 'Do you have a wife or girlfriend?'

'No.'

'When you do I bet she'll love you like I loved Jason. I'd like some coffee.'

'Okay, lovely lady. Coffee it is. Did you know the other people he was in the army with?'

'Yes.'

'Did you like them?'

230

'Some of them. Gabriel was in love with Michael Carmichael and we saw him occasionally and Michael and Jason used to have long discussions in the kitchen.'

'What about?'

'I don't know really. It was sort of secret and sometimes they would argue.'

'What about Malcom Wright?'

'I didn't like him. He used to try it on but when I said I would tell Jason he would stop. I don't think he liked Jason really but had to do what Jason told him.'

'What sort of things?'

'I don't know really. When I asked, Jason told me to forget about it. It was the only times Jason was, well, annoyed with me so I didn't ask.'

'What did you think it was?'

Patsy just stared at me.

'You know don't you?'

'Probably.' She was weighing up what she was going to tell me. 'Gabriel won't get into trouble?'

'No, not from me.'

Again she went into thinking mode. 'Gabriel trusts you.'

'Oh, I am pleased.'

'He wouldn't have done it if it hadn't been for Michael.'

'What wouldn't he have done?'

She bit her bottom lip.

'They were smuggling drugs from Afghanistan.'

'That's pretty dangerous.' She went to speak. 'No, Patsy I won't tell.' She smiled a smile of relief. She had wanted to unburden herself and she was now relieved. Funny really.

She was silent, looking at me; she knew something else and wanted to tell me.

'Are you going to tell me, Patsy?'

She nodded. 'Some women were murdered and Jason thought Major Carmichael did it.'

'Yes.'

'But it wasn't the major, it was Wright.'

'How do you know?'

'Gabriel told me.'

'So Gabriel knew?'

'Yes.'

'How?'

'Wright was bragging, the way he does.'

'Gabriel didn't know what to do so I told him to tell you.'

'It's okay Patsy. He told me.'

'Will he go to prison?'

I knew she was talking about Gabriel.

'Yes, but he will be all right.' Patsy nodded. 'Now drink your coffee.'

Patsy smiled her quiet smile and obediently sipped the coffee.

I paid and took her back across the road to the hospital. Now we had to part. She threw her arms around me and kissed me on the lips. Her hands were clasped behind my neck.

'Thank you. Oh, thank you. I feel so much better now I have told you.' She paused, looking at me. 'This has been the best time I've had since Jason died. Talking about him to you has been fantastic. You're so easy to talk to that I can say anything to you. I'm going home now and I'll be a teacher and when I am, if you don't have a permanent lady by then, I'm coming back for you.' She let go of me, turned and disappeared into the hospital. I might say her step was jaunty and I felt extraordinary. I don't know what had gone on in her head but clearly she'd got some things into per-spective. I think I'd helped somebody even if it didn't help the case. I had that very positive feeling like when Dad got through Reading Book 1 in prison. Yes, Patsy O'Donnell, you go and be a teacher and have days that are just great because you've helped somebody and I'll do what I can for your brother.

48

When I got back to Earls Court nick, the interview was still in progress, so I grabbed a coffee and sat in the office area that had been allocated to Kitty and her team, four of them. DC Debora Mackenzie was toiling to gather background information on Malcolm Wright. She had some, such as the fact that he'd been in residential care from the age of five and had also been fostered twice. Debora had also found out that both Jason Phillips and Malcolm Wright had been in the same lodgings, having left the same residential home a year apart. Wright was older by a year and when Jase went to the Army Foundation College just before he was seventeen Malcolm Wright joined the school of infantry for basic training. So this confirmed what we'd been told by Gil Hibberd. Outside of the basic facts, however, Debora was having problems getting details. She'd discovered that Wright had been trouble from about the age of ten but not enough for any serious charges. He'd also made the rank of lance corporal but been reduced to private again, but she had no detail as to why. Here was a very frustrated detective constable.

I was thinking of giving Debora some help when Kitty came in. She looked like death. Her face was sheet white. Even her lips were bloodless and she had deep, dark rings around her eyes. I went to her and she clung to me and broke down. She was sobbing. The office went deathly silent and then as if by some signal, the people in the office left

233

and we stood locked together with sobs racking her body. Slowly they subsided and she broke away. I was staggered; this was one tough lady. What had happened in there?

'Where the fuck did you go, you bastard?' Her attack was vicious. 'Men: all the fucking same. They disappear when you need them most.' She hunted in her handbag. I gave her a handkerchief. That was me out of handkerchiefs. The attack eased.

'That's my girl. Sit down here. Let me get you a coffee.'

She looked at me, swaying, and I thought she was going to faint. I put my hand out and she took it. I then led her to a chair and she sat. She put her elbows on the desk and her head in her hands. She was crying again but now gently. I went to the coffee pot at the side of the room and as I poured it, Gaygan came in. He was wiping his mouth with a paper towel. He was distinctly green. I caught him and sat him down before he fainted.

'Christ! What happened?'

Neither of them said anything.

'Somebody bloody talk to me!'

Kitty looked up. 'He killed eleven, not including Celia.' She paused and gathered herself. 'Some are just where he left them waiting to be found. It was three in Iraq and then there was the one in Washington.'

I pulled a chair up and turned her chair so she was facing me with my knees not quite touching hers. Her hands were in her lap and she was looking at them. 'Okay, Inspector, talk. Overview. No detail.' I pumped out the words, crisp and clear. I had to cut through the emotion. I needed a picture but more than that I needed her to get her head straight.

'He killed twelve women. Each of them had been friends of somebody who had gone out with Jason Phillips, usually their boss or the leader of the group. The second factor was they were rich. Wright's mother was rich. His father died and his mother had this series of boyfriends and they didn't hide what they were doing from him. She posed for porno pictures, she was shaved for that and that is probably a link to Phillips, and he, you know, Wright was sometimes involved in the porno. Social services took him into care when he was about five. He went back to his mother for about six months when he was seven. It was at this time that he was physically abused.'

'Abused?'

Kitty looked at the floor. She was shaking her head.

'Kitty, do I need to know or not?'

'No, you don't need to know, but I'm going to bloody tell you.' Her face was scrunched up as if she was crying or going to cry but she was ice cold. I needed to stay calm, neutral and supportive but not show sympathy. 'The bitch sucked him – his own mother – and they took photos and paid her. When he told us he loved it, telling us, that's where the earring thing came from, he learned it from his mother. They also got him to do it to men. Perverted pae-dophiles took pictures. They did other things.' Now she started to cry again, deep racking sobs. I was fighting my emotions; I bit my lower lip and blood ran down inside. I had to stay supportive and calm.

'They turned a little boy into a monster and he was taken back into care. It was the girl thing that pushed Wright over the top. In the home he raped a few of the small girls and got them to give him oral sex. There are some damaged women out there because of what his mother did to him. His mother died of an overdose soon after that but he didn't know that until he was sixteen. Phillips was in the same home as him. They left at the same time; well, about four months apart.' She stopped and looked at me.

I nodded and said very gently, 'Go on.'

'Phillips had all the girls. He was a sporting hero, primarily swimming but he was good at everything he did: football,

235

athletics, schoolwork and most of all, girls. Wright wanted revenge on rich women and he wanted Phillips to be blamed. Your suggestion about Phillips' girlfriends opened the gates. He saw Jason Phillips as the person who had abused his mother. It's totally irrational but he sees it that way. He knew about the body hair thing so he did that to his victims. They thought it was a sex game thing. He then sexually abused them in the same way he'd seen men abuse his mother. He didn't just tell us, he gave details of the suffering he inflicted.' She stopped. She was visualising what Wright had said and she shivered. 'He's convinced that was what Phillips was doing to his girlfriends. He beat them with a cane because he saw men do that to his mother and he said she liked it. He clearly loved doing it. He then strangled them. He killed them so Phillips would be blamed but why strangulation he didn't or couldn't tell us. When it was raised he started to gag as if he was being strangled. I reckon that's what happened to him as a kid. That's the summary, you bastard.' Her voice was now quiet and balanced. The pain and venom had subsided. She needed to let it out and I was there to accept it.

'Thank you, Inspector. Will you get more information?'

'No, I think we've enough, no bloody thanks to you.' She smiled a weak smile and shook her head. She was thanking me for being there. It wasn't what the words said but that's what they meant. It seemed they had all the information they were likely to get and enough to ensure there would be a trial and maybe enough for a conviction.

I just sat there. People started to return. She looked up at me and I gave her a paper handkerchief from a box on a cabinet. She dried her face and gave another very weak smile. Embarrassment?

'I'm sorry, Jake. Thank you for coping with me,' she said then stood up and I stood too. She threw her arms around me and I held her. She was sobbing, but eventually it died down and she was breathing normally again.

236

'Okay, lovely?'

'I love you, you miserable bastard,' she said and left the room, a wet tissue to her face.

I went over to Gaygan. He'd been listening. 'You okay?'

'Not really, Jake. It wasn't what he said or did; it was that he got so much pleasure out of telling us. He was proud of what he'd done. He didn't even seem to think it was wrong.' Gaygan shut his eyes. He was emotionally exhausted. The room was silent.

'Can I do anything for you?'

He opened his eyes. 'She was brilliant in there. She held it together. She did all the things she was supposed to do. She asked him open questions, got him talking and sought clarification about what he'd said. She used what he'd said to move the interview forward and open up avenues for more information. She paraphrased and summarised, supported and challenged. She was just brilliant. She's always been good but since she's worked with you she, she, she's just brilliant.'

What do you say? 'That's great, Gaygan. Can I get you a coffee?'

He smiled. 'Definitely not.' He smiled a bigger smile. 'I'll get one for you.' He paused, smiled then said, 'You've got her back on an even keel, Jake. Thank you. We can now nail the bastard.' This was the hidden Gaygan speaking, firm and assertive.

I hadn't done anything, so I sat and sipped my coffee. What was clear was that Gaygan had much more than just admiration for his inspector.

49

Kitty came back ten minutes later with repaired makeup and her hair tidy. She was in balance, the horror that she had listened to was behind her and I strongly suspected she would never be pulled down again in a similar situation. Kitty and Gaygan chatted about what they needed now. It seemed they just needed Wright to say he would plead guilty and he would be nailed. Kitty went through it with me and when we arrived at the subject of entering a plea, they both just stared at me.

'What?'

'It's up to you.'

'What is?'

'Convincing him to plead guilty.'

'That's a bit premature isn't it?'

'No. We reckon if he says it here it'll happen, he will plead and there won't be a trial.'

'Take me through why you don't want a trial.'

'Apart from obvious such as the cost and fickleness of juries and all the usual stuff, all we really have is a confession. No rock solid evidence, no fingerprints, no DNA, no weapons, no eyewitnesses. The only thing we can nail him on is the Celia killing and only because Gabriel was also involved so that is dicky. If we just go with that the smart defence will find a way of screwing it.'

'Okay, I'll give it a go but Keith Todd may scupper it.' I then had to think of an approach and said to Kitty as we were walking back to the interview room, 'Don't switch on the tapes.'

She shrugged, but followed the instruction when we were inside. I took the left-hand seat opposite Wright while she went to the recorder and flicked some switches. The red light was on – power – but no green, so not operational. She then sat to the right of me opposite Keith. Malcolm Wright and Keith were looking at me expectantly. I had no idea what they expected. Keith looked like he'd been blown up by a bomb but Wright was just tense.

'Malcolm, you know me and I'm going to make a statement to you and I'm going to ask you to make a decision. Is that okay?'

He looked at Keith. Keith nodded.

'Yes, s'pose.'

'Malcolm, I'm going to say this only once. Are you listening?'

'Yes.'

'You've told us about the murders and we've that on tape and we'll write it up and get you to sign it. Do you understand?' I was using the old 'get them saying yes' trick.

'Yes.'

'We'll forward what we have to the Crown Prosecution Service. We expect them to tell us to charge you with murder. Do you also expect that?'

'Yeah, I s'pose.'

'We've a witness in Gabriel Holt who will be tried as an accomplice in the murder of Corporal Celia Foley. Is that clear?'

'Yeah.'

'There's a powerful gang and political forces out there.' I paused. I let the implications sink in. 'Jase was murdered in Peasmarsh Prison.' I paused again. I hoped he would put two and two together and make four. I was silently praying that Keith would stay silent. 'We want you to plead guilty to the serial killings. You forget all about the Gabriel–Michael relationship. If you want to talk drugs fine, but Jase was 'the man' and you were 'the doer'. No Michael involvement.' I let that sink in. 'Do you understand?'

'Yeah, I want to stay alive. What will I get?'

Good, he realised he was in danger of being assassinated.

'You'll go down for life maybe in a nut house; it depends on the shrinks. Okay?'

'S'pose.'

'Good, and now comes the important bit. Are you listening?' He nodded. 'Good.' I paused and he was looking at me and listening, I glance at Keith. He was focused on me. 'If you decide to plead not guilty, I will kill you.'

Keith went to speak. I looked at the tape recorder and he saw it was off. I saw realisation in his eyes. 'Have you got that, Malcolm?' He was totally focused on me. He nodded. 'If I can't get to you I'll pull some strings and you'll go to Peasmarsh Prison compliments of the Home Secretary and I've a couple of friends in there who will do the job for a transfer to an open prison and a shorter sentence, compliments of the Home Secretary. Okay?'

He nodded.

'You understand?'

He nodded. 'You'll kill me, Captain.'

'I'm going to turn the tape machine on and Inspector Halloway will ask you a couple of questions and wrap this up. It's now up to you. Understand?'

'Yes, Captain. I'm gonna plead guilty, sir.'

'You're going to have a top barrister, Sir Nicolas Ross, and you can live happily ever after even if in rather confined circumstances.'

Keith looked at the ceiling and shook his head and then looked back at me, wearing an expression that said everything I wanted it to say. I then switched on the tape recorders. Kitty did the introductions for the tape and then told

Wright about writing up the information and giving him a copy of the recording. She asked Wright whether he understood and whether he committed the killings. He said he did. And that he would plead guilty in court. He said he would.

50

Kitty, Gaygan and I went to the canteen.

'It's all over. I'm out now,' I told them.

'That business about killing Wright...' Kitty paused then said, 'Well?'

'Well what?'

'Would you kill him?'

'I won't need to. If he stands up in court and pleads not guilty he's a dead man. I'm out. I believe I'm safe because I'm known as safe and it's known that I've some protection but you're not safe. Never be associated with any reporter, enquiry or report on this, or the amber risk-rating you now have will turn red.'

'What are you saying, Jake? I'm confused.'

'You've a killer who is about to go into remand for a while and will plead guilty. You've an accessory that you'll hide away. Eventually, they'll appear in court or perhaps not – it depends whether The Family let them appear.'

'You're saying The Family will assassinate them.'

'"May" not "will". Think about this; Gabriel had an affair with Michael Carmichael. That mustn't come out. Will the prosecution probe in to this when Gabriel is on the stand? If the risk is real then Gabriel is a dead man. It depends who the prosecution barrister is and I think that will be a Family person, so Gabriel will be okay.'

'You mean the prosecution won't ask questions that expose Carmichael?'

'Spot on.'

'What about the defence?'

'Sir Nicolas Ross knows the score and probably doesn't need that sleaze to defend Wright.'

'But that depends on Sir Nicolas. What if Wright changes barristers?'

'Then Wright is dead. Wright, Gabriel and Jase were in a drug-running business with Carmichael. The Carmichael element mustn't come out. Wright, the serial killer, was close to Carmichael and that mustn't come out. In short, any risk whatsoever that Michael Carmichael's name is associated with this must be eliminated. So, not only Wright and Gabriel are at risk, you and your team are at risk, Kitty, you have information dangerous to The Family.' Kitty and Gaygan were looking horrified. 'There'll be investigative journalists already looking for a story. There'll be true crime writers looking for a story. There are soldiers out there and one or two may want to tell a story, not understanding how risky that is. The Family will be applying pressure but if Wright were to die the prime information source is blocked and everything becomes second-hand.'

'You don't think Wright will make trial do you, Jake?'

'No, Kitty. I'd bet a grand or even fifty grand that Wright doesn't make trial. In fact, I'm surprised he's still alive.'

'Why do you think he's still alive then?'

'Either they wanted to use him for something, to take the hit for the killings away from Carmichael, or he knows something that they want to know or he knows something they don't want revealed and he's hidden it somewhere like Gabriel did.'

'So, are you saying he's not really the serial killer?'

'Good lord, no! I'm saying The Family thought Carmichael was the killer and wanted a fall guy. That Wright is the killer is a bonus.'

'What information might he have?'

243

'Absolutely no idea but, and here is the dangerous thing, if he does know something and he tries to use it as a bargaining chip then we're in a whole new ballgame. I've looked through everything we have on him. There was a lot of shit but I found nothing that he can use against The Family but that doesn't mean much. He could have ferreted stuff away.'

51

I was back with Sir Nicolas Ross, doing what I always did for him, gathering information that could be used to defend his clients, and we spent nearly half a day going over the Wright case. This was an extraordinarily long time for him on a case and we worked through the information of how the ball may bounce and how he would deflect it into the long grass. After nearly three hours of discussion, his phone rang. It was Vera. Apparently, Rupert Carmichael wanted to talk to me again and was inviting me to come to lunch in the Churchill Room at his club, The Carlton Club. I told Vera that I agreed.

I walked from the Strand, through Charing Cross and up Pall Mall, about three quarters of a mile through some old, historic and expensive parts of London. I was spot on time and was shown into a large lounge with deep leather chairs where we could chat, have a drink and order lunch.

'Welcome, Jake. It's so good to see you again.'

'Good afternoon, Rupert.'

A number of members looked over their glasses, both the ones they were wearing and the ones from which they were drinking. We shook hands and he led the way to a quiet corner where two leather armchairs were facing a wall with a table in front of them. As we sat down a member of staff quietly approached and Rupert Carmichael ordered a Tanqueray and tonic with ice and lemon and a brandy and ginger for himself. This was a man who remembered detail.

'Thank you, Your Grace,' said the waiter and backed away with a slight inclination of his head. Oh, what it is to be among wealthy and powerful nobility, even if they were criminals. I don't suppose he saw himself as a criminal. Criminals for him were probably people who wore striped jumpers and carried bags that said swag on them. The waiter returned in a twinkling with the drinks and another young man gave us menus that we left on the table. The room was quiet. There were people talking but the nature of the furniture arrangements, the heavy drapes, décor and furnishings, were such as to deaden sound, so each of the small groups were private without intrusive barriers.

'To business, Jake. Do we have a problem with the two miscreants?'

To call two murderers miscreants did seem to underplay it a bit considering one of them had killed at least twelve women whom he'd raped and tortured, drugged and strangled. Hardly a miscreant, but it depended on your starting point I supposed.

'They'll both plead guilty but they're very different. Gabriel Holt will toe the line; he's not basically a criminal. Wright, on the other hand, is a sociopath; he has no values, no honour. He says he'll plead guilty and I've warned him of the consequences of not doing as he's agreed.'

'The consequences are, Jake?'

'I told him I'd kill him.'

'Does he believe you?'

'He did at the time, but who knows now.'

'So he could be trouble?'

'Could be.'

'What does he know?'

'Everything, Rupert.'

'By everything you mean what?'

'He was active for Michael and Jase in the drugs business.

He knows who does what, where and how. He knew about Michael's relationship with Gabriel Holt.'

'Wright was definitely the killer?'

'Yes, Rupert.'

'You told him you'd kill him and he believed you?'

'At the time, yes, Rupert.'

'At that time. You think he might talk?'

'I think it's a possibility.'

Rupert nodded his head.

'But Holt isn't going to be a problem. He'll just do his time?' The Earl's well-paced upper-class pronunciation sought absolute assurance.

'Yes, Rupert.'

He smiled and nodded. He trusted my judgement. 'What are you having for lunch then, Jake?' he asked and his tone of voice had changed from business to that of a friend. I knew a decision had been made but I could only guess at it. I didn't think Wright would make a hearing. I hoped I'd saved Gabriel, though; I suspected both had been at risk when I came in.

The luncheon menu had such delights as steak and kidney pudding, and treacle sponge and custard, so that was what I ordered, with a lager. We sat and chatted about politics and football and generally had a pleasant lunch. Then, as we sipped our coffee and nibbled the petit fours, Rupert said, 'Have you thought any more about joining me, Jake? I need someone to guard my arse and be an advisor I can trust.' So *consigliare* was on the table.

'It depends on the business, Rupert.'

'Yes, I suppose it does.'

'But the bigger problem is, Rupert, I'd have to call you sir.'

He laughed. 'It's so rare that anybody has turned down a job that I've offered them; in fact, you're the only one. It tells me you're exactly what I need, but one day, Jake, one

247

day you'll work for me and I'm only a phone call away. Brandy?'

'No thank you, Rupert. I have to walk back to the office.'

He smiled, we shook hands and I left to walk down Pall Mall, through Charing Cross, onto the Strand and into Sir Nicolas's chambers to see Gillian still introducing the worst criminals in England who weren't working for Rupert Carmichael – Earl of Charnforth, Head of The Family, the top criminal in the country – to their defence barrister.

52

I had a call from the CPS telling me that the trial would start the following Wednesday at 10.00 a.m. and they wanted me at their offices to make certain all the beans were in a row. I wasn't sure if I had to be there, but it was confirmed; the prosecution had me down as a witness. I'd wriggled but to no avail. I was on the hook.

The offices of the CPS were, as one might expect, busy. The receptionist was one of those people who has an amazing ability to cope with chaos and still make things work smoothly and remain calm when all about them were definitely not. She smiled at me; I showed her my piece of paper and received an instruction to sit. She did this so competently and, I must say, forcefully but politely that I did just as I was told.

Petal King came down to collect me. 'Good morning, Jake. I'm pleased you're now out of the clink. Come upstairs and we can go through this case.'

'I'm pleased to see you as well, Petal. Are you the prosecutor?'

'No, Peter Traeger is but we're all close here, almost a family you might say.'

So I was right; she was Family and I think she thought I was as well. When she came to visit me in prison I knew she was Family and I expected Family barristers at this hearing and trial. The tentacles were long and far-reaching. I wondered if the judge would be Family too.

We arrived at an office upstairs and it was clear that this was the seat of the chaos downstairs. There were bundles of papers everywhere. Peter Traeger left his desk, shook my hand and said, 'Good of you to come, Jake. Come in, please, have a seat.'

I sat.

'You've met Petal before. What I want to do is make sure we all know what's going on. The focus will only be on the serial killings and the defendant, Malcolm Wright. Let me run through how I envisage the questioning going, if it goes to trial. I'll bring you on as the first prosecution witness as you were in at the beginning in Iraq. We recognise there are some problems as your Sergeant Billinghurst is no longer with us. It may be better if you just confirm she's dead and be careful on cross examination so that you minimise the facts and omit that you were also shot by the same person and that he's dead. It could open up a whole can of worms. I'll take you through the two originally known killings in Iraq, the narrowing down of the suspects and the identification of just two at the end, and the fact that they both have confessed during questioning by Detective Inspector Halloway.'

'Are you saying there will be a trial?'

'Both the defendants are going to plead guilty. So we believe both will go to the Crown Court for sentencing. We would like you to stand by in case there's a change in the plea or the judge decides to take some evidence.'

From the way he spoke he didn't expect the judge to take evidence but he didn't tap the side of his nose. He talked through the inquiry, checked and tested some things and was satisfied that if it did go for trial the defence would go for insanity and that's what the psychiatrists' reports said, but, as he told me, there's many a slip between cup and lip. His speech was also scattered with such proverbs, similes and metaphors. I reckoned it was Broadmoor for Malcolm Wright if and only if he survived that long.

53

The day came and as I left St Paul's tube station for the Old Bailey, my mobile rang – well, they don't ring these days; they play tunes and jingles but mine just makes an aggravating noise and it was like that when I got it. I'd been meaning to do something about it but never had. It was Kitty. Would I go to the Scrubs urgently? So I got on a train to East Acton. The message was simple – Malcolm Wright was dead. No surprise there then.

I went to the visitors' centre as advised. There, Gaygan met me and a prison officer escorted us to a dining area. The place was alive with people and Wright was very dead. There were at least six from SOCO, four uniformed police officers and Kitty was there with a large man in black – well, a large black man in black. Kitty introduced us. He was Superintendent Jerome Taylor.

'I'm not sure why you're here, Mr Robinson.'

'Nor am I.'

'As an advisor to me,' said Kitty. 'Jake has particular experience and knowledge of murder in prisons and he has particular knowledge of the Wright case.'

'If you think he'd be useful, Chief Inspector.'

'So you've been promoted, Kitty. Congratulations.'

'Thank you, Jake.'

'Fill me in.'

'It's one of those impossible situations. Wright was getting ready to leave for the Bailey. He was to have a late breakfast. The dining room was clear. He went up to the counter. As food was placed on his tray there' – she pointed to the serving counter where there were a cluster of people in white coveralls – 'there was a shot. Wright went down with a bullet in his chest.

'We have the gun and everybody who was in the kitchen and the server, and that's it so far. The forensic team is working but the first indications are absolutely nothing. Each of the people who were in here have been separated and all we have from the interviews is "saw a flash, heard a bang and a man was dead". It's a classic reversal of the three monkeys situation so far. I saw something, I heard something and I'm talking but I'm actually saying nothing.'

'And that's how it'll continue. Anybody who talks is a dead man unless you can offer anonymity and a new life with a new name. Can I see the body?'

I was taken to the body at the front of the servery. Wright was lying on his back covered with a sheet. A woman in a white forensic suit lifted the sheet. The bullet had hit his chest and from the amount of blood, had hit his heart.

I asked the forensic woman, 'Large calibre weapon, probably a forty five and a dum-dum bullet?'

'That's what we think, sir.'

'Fired by a handgun or revolver, probably six feet or less away?'

'Revolver, sir. We think two metres. Yes, sir.'

It's odd how I think in feet and inches. I suppose that comes from working with an uncle of mine who was a carpenter when on holiday from school. I can imagine feet and inches but while all the calculations in school were done in metric I couldn't visualise it. Anyway, I'm English and my speedometer reads in miles per hour and road signs are in real measurements.

'Whoever fired was standing directly behind the prisoner serving food. The counter is a metre wide, the server probably another fifty centimetres, then, say, another fifty centimetres to the weapon, so two metres. So, yes, about six feet and yes, it was an old, Second World War, point four five revolver. It contained three other bullets all hollow point.'

'The server deafened?'

'Temporarily, yes, sir.'

'And the shooter?'

'Nobody else, sir.'

'Found the earplugs?'

'Sorry, sir?'

'Big bang in closed space, often but not necessarily some temporary deafness.'

'Right, sir.'

'Probably used wax because it can be dropped into a hot pan and this was planned so you won't find the plugs, but you might find some odd wax on the hairs in the ears.'

'Yes, sir. I'll tell the boss.' She shot away to an older man.

'Congratulations, Mr Robinson,' said Superintendent Taylor. 'What's your background?'

'RMP and MI5.'

'I see. A diverse pedigree.'

A woman was checking ears with a swab and light and putting her findings into tubes that a police constable was writing on.

'What do you reckon, Jake?' asked Kitty.

'Well, the gun had to be smuggled in. Difficult. Probably not someone visiting a prisoner but if it was brought in that way it wasn't given to the killer.'

'So you're thinking staff?'

'Big chunk of metal, a point four five revolver. Say, seven inches long by five inches deep and weighing about two and a half pounds. Staff or supplier is my guess. More likely in bits. Two and a half pounds of metal can be difficult but broken down each piece is easier. This was special for this job so it'll be untraceable.'

Kitty and her team and the big superintendent were listening.

'This was a professional hit so the killer had to be briefed. The questions are: what visitors did each of the people in this kitchen have and which of them would be capable of delivering such a briefing? Who, of them, has the skill to shoot one of those beasts accurately, one bullet, not a difficult shot, but not one for someone unpractised? Then there's the motivation, either reward or threat. Guard your arse, Kitty. This is a contract killing ordered by some very powerful people. Was Wright going to spill the beans?'

'I think so, Jake,' said Gaygan. 'Some *Sun* reporter thinks he'd a sniff of something.'

'Kitty, I suggest you get Rob to visit him.'

The SOCO woman was putting the sheet back over Wright.

'What else have you got?' I asked.

The man behind her, whom I assumed was the boss she'd referred to, replied, 'We've three bullets and a spent cartridge case. We've seven fingerprints.'

'That's great. Surprising but great.' But I could see they were not happy. 'But?'

The SOCO man replied. 'We've a quick scan set. It seems each of the prints are different'

'You mean you think seven different people handled the bullets?'

'Well, we may be wrong but that's unlikely and when we've done the comparisons with the database it may give us a match.'

'But you're not hopeful?'

'If this is, as you suggested, a professionally set-up killing, I doubt it.'

'What about the gun?'

'First scan, as clean as a whistle. Maybe, just maybe, we'll get something at the lab.'

'Anything else?'

'Only the shirt of the prisoner who was serving. It had cordite burns.'

'Cordite?'

'These look like very old bullets.'

'The prisoner serving, the shooter was up close to him, what does he say?'

'Whatcha say?' mimicked Kitty, holding a cupped hand to her ear.

I laughed. 'Good one, Kitty.'

The big man in black was not amused.

Kitty's new inspector answered. 'He says he's no idea who was behind him and can he have a hearing aid and can he sue the prison?'

'God, this is frustrating,' said Kitty.

'Have you also checked the prison officers who were in here?'

The superintendent was about to speak when Kitty cut across him. 'Yes, Jake. Reading about the Peasmarsh job was a good learning experience.'

'I think you should have them all charged with obstruction and accessory to murder.'

'If only we could,' said the superintendent. 'We'll more likely end up with some civil action for exposing them to loud bangs and frightening them with dead bodies.' There was general cynical agreement.

'Well, I don't like prisons so I'll be away, but if you want to talk you know where I am.'

'It was good to meet you, Jake.' The big man held out his hand. We shook. 'Spent some time in prisons have you?'

'Unfortunately I have, but I was fitted up, Gov.' I laughed and he didn't know whether to believe me. That was that then. I could go on a well-deserved holiday to Scotland.

Jake Robinson will return in *Saving A Lady*.

Saving a Lady

Jake Robinson was in bed wrapped round Sorcha, a beautiful Nordic girl. He was enjoying a dirty weekend with her in Ullapool on Loch Broom. He had no idea of the drama unfolding in the Home Office.

In the anteroom leading to the Home Secretary's offices, The Long Room, senior police officers gathered.

Detective Superintendent Alan Peterson, Head of the Kidnap Unit was desperately trying to keep still and maintain his composure as he waited in the long anteroom. He'd never met the Home Secretary, but he had heard about the acid that he could drip upon anybody that displeased him.

Detective Chief Inspector Andrew Lankford knew he was the man in the hot seat. He looked at the photos of past Home Secretaries that decorated the walls and trembled slightly, but he didn't know why this kidnap was so important that the Home Secretary would be involved. He had been the senior investigating officer and had found absolutely nothing. That was the problem: no evidence of a break-in to the convent, no evidence of a struggle. The nun's bed had been slept in. The only evidence that anybody had been in the room was the fingerprints and DNA of Sister Veronica. Just no Sister Veronica. He hadn't been informed that Sister Veronica was Annabelle Mabry, the sister of the Home Secretary. There were lots of street cameras but in the fateful period between Compline that finished at about 10.00 p.m. and Lauds that started at 6.00 a.m. there was nothing on the street cameras. Sister Veronica had just disappeared.

Sir Martin Ashworth, the commissioner of the metropolitan police, seemed quite relaxed. He had regular contact with the Home Secretary. It had never been anything of a personal nature, just business, and he felt the Home Secretary trusted him or at least respected him as the head of the most powerful police force in the country. He itched slightly, however, that Sir Barrow Jones was to be involved. Such an unaccountable unit as the special unit of MI5 should not exist in a democracy built on freedom and the law.

Sir Barrow Jones, head of the special unit of MI5, was in a car that had been sent for him, but he had no idea what this was about. He could only guess that it was very serious. His unit was never engaged unless there was a threat to the safety of the United Kingdom or there was a very special job that the government wanted done but they didn't want to know how the job was done or who did it, and when done the particular minister of the government didn't want to know such a job had ever been done by anybody at any time.

Only Sir Barrow Jones knew that the Home Secretary had asked for Jake Robinson to be involved, but why, he didn't know.